"**May I have this dance?**"

Morgan West would have known the voice anywhere, even here in a Sea Cliff mansion in the middle of an elegant, black-tie party. Rather numbly, she looked up to meet the laughing green eyes of the most famous—and infamous—cat burglar in the world.

Quinn.

He was dressed for the party, a handsome heartbreaker in a stark black dinner jacket. His fair hair gleamed as he bowed very slightly with exquisite grace before her, and Morgan knew without doubt that at least half the female eyes in the crowded ballroom were fixed on him.

The other half just hadn't seen him yet.

WHAT ARE *LOVESWEPT* ROMANCES?

They are stories of true romance and touching emotion. We believe those two very important ingredients are constants in our highly sensual and very believable stories in the LOVESWEPT line. Our goal is to give you, the reader, stories of consistently high quality that may sometimes make you laugh, sometimes make you cry, but are always fresh and creative and contain many delightful surprises within their pages.

Most romance fans read an enormous number of books. Those they truly love, they keep. Others may be traded with friends and soon forgotten. We hope that each LOVESWEPT romance will be a treasure—a "keeper." We will always try to publish

LOVE STORIES YOU'LL NEVER FORGET
BY AUTHORS YOU'LL ALWAYS REMEMBER

The Editors

Men of Mysteries Past

ALL FOR QUINN

KAY HOOPER

BANTAM BOOKS

NEW YORK · TORONTO · LONDON · SYDNEY · AUCKLAND

ALL FOR QUINN

A Bantam Book / August 1993

*Great things are done
when men and mountains meet.*
—WILLIAM BLAKE

PROLOGUE

The cold fog drifting over the bay began to obscure the distant, hulking outline of Alcatraz, and Quinn was glad. Though it was no longer a place where dangerous criminals were held, the defunct prison and its lonely island continued to be a stark, visible reminder of the price demanded of those who chose to be lawless.

Quinn didn't need the reminder.

Still, as he turned up the collar of his jacket and dug his hands into the pockets, he watched the rocky island until the mist enveloped it and rendered it invisible. It was an eerie sight, the fog creeping over the water toward him while, behind him, the moonlight gleamed down on the city. At least it did right now, which was sometime after midnight. In another hour, Quinn thought, he probably wouldn't be able to see his hand in front of his face.

He was beginning to really like this city.

"Why the hell are we meeting here?"

Quinn had been aware of the other person's presence before he heard or saw anything, so the low voice didn't surprise him. "I thought it was rather apt," he murmured in response. "Before the fog rolled in, Alcatraz was shining like a beacon in the moonlight."

Jared Chavalier sighed. "Are you getting edgy? You, Alex?" His voice held a very slight note of mockery.

Quinn turned his back on the aged, mist-enshrouded prison and looked at his companion. "No, but I'll be glad when this is over. I'd forgotten how long the nights get."

"Your choice," Jared reminded him.

"Yeah, I know."

Jared had keen eyes, and the moon was still visible hanging low over the city, so he was able to see the lean face of his brother clearly. "Is your shoulder bothering you?" he asked a bit roughly.

Quinn shrugged, the movement easy and showing no sign of the damage a bullet had caused a couple of weeks previously. "No. You know I'm a quick healer."

"Even for a quick healer, that was a nasty wound. You probably should have stayed at Morgan's longer than a few days."

"No," Quinn said. "I shouldn't have done that."

After a moment Jared said, "So, Max was right."

"About what?"

"Don't be deliberately dense, Alex."

Quinn resisted the impulse to ask if he could be

accidentally dense. "Max is very perceptive—but he isn't always right. As for Morgan, let's just say that I have enough common sense for both of us."

"And no time for romance?"

"And no time for romance." Quinn wondered, not for the first time, if becoming such an accomplished liar had been a good thing or a bad one. It might have kept his skin intact a bit longer, he thought, but sooner or later it was all going to catch up with him—and a great many people would no doubt be furious at him.

Jared seemed to be thinking along the same lines.

"We've been amazingly lucky so far," he said. "But you really can't afford to get in any deeper with Morgan."

"I know that."

"She knows too much."

Quinn drew a deep breath, but kept his voice light. "Pardon me for not thinking too clearly when I was bleeding. I'll try to do better next time."

"I'm not blaming you for that."

"Too kind."

Jared swore roughly. "Look, all I'm saying is that we're running out of time. You really *don't* have the leisure—or the right—to pull any woman into a situation like this, especially when you're dealing with someone as deadly as Nightshade."

Calmer now, Quinn said quietly, "Yes. You're right, I know that. And I am trying."

Somewhat mollified, Jared asked, "Is that why you

didn't make an appearance at the private showing to-night? To avoid Morgan?"

Instead of answering that, Quinn said, "I saw an impressive number of limos and fancy cars arriving at the museum. The showing was a success, I gather?"

"In spades. And since there were enough armed guards to make even a moronic thief think twice, no trouble."

Quinn nodded. "The exhibit opens to the public next Friday. I think we both agree that the sooner we lure Nightshade into the trap, the better. If we let him, he could well wait for the next two months and make his move when we've relaxed our guard."

"I'd rather not have to haunt the museum for the next two months," Jared said politely. "Since I'm get-ting married later today, I'd really like to use at least part of my leave time for an extended honeymoon. Dani doesn't mind that we have to stay here in San Francisco indefinitely, but it would be nice if I didn't have to work all these odd hours. So the sooner we wrap this up, the happier I'll be."

"I imagine so. By the way, don't be surprised if you happen to see me in the church today."

"Alex—"

"Not openly," Quinn soothed, his voice calm. "But I've cased the building and there's a place where I can watch and listen. I missed your first wedding to Dani; I want to be there for this one."

Jared didn't say anything for a moment, and when

he did, his comment was dry. "Doesn't it strike you as indecent to be casing a church?"

"Not when my brother's getting married there," Quinn replied unrepentantly.

Jared laughed. "All right, but for God's sake be careful."

"I'm always careful."

That solemn statement was so wide of the mark that Jared could only shake his head. "Sure you are."

"I am. And I plan to be very, very careful during the next step of my plan."

"Which is?" Jared inquired somewhat wearily.

"Well, hunting by night hasn't earned me much except a bullet. I think it's time I tried a more direct approach."

Jared sighed. "I've got a feeling I won't like this."

"No, probably not." Quinn's even white teeth showed in a sudden grin. "But I will."

A certain man went down from Jerusalem to Jericho and fell among thieves.

—LUKE 10:30

ONE

"May I have this dance?"

Morgan West would have known the voice anywhere, even here in a Sea Cliff mansion in the middle of an elegant, black-tie party. Rather numbly, she looked up to meet the laughing green eyes of the most famous—and infamous—cat burglar in the world.

Quinn.

He was dressed for the party, a handsome heartbreaker in a stark black dinner jacket. His fair hair gleamed as he bowed very slightly with exquisite grace before her, and Morgan knew without doubt that at least half the female eyes in the crowded ballroom were fixed on him.

The other half just hadn't seen him yet.

"Oh, God," she murmured.

Quinn lifted her drink from her hand and set it on a nearby table. "As I believe I've told you once before, Morgana—not nearly," he said nonchalantly.

As he led her out onto the dance floor, Morgan told herself she certainly didn't want to make a scene. That was why she wasn't resisting him, of course. And it was also why she fixed a pleasantly noncommittal smile on her face despite the fact that her heart was going like a trip-hammer.

"What are you doing here?" she demanded in a low, fierce voice.

"I'm dancing with the most beautiful woman in the room," he replied, suiting action to words as he drew her into his arms and began moving to the music, which was slow and dreamy.

Morgan refused to be flattered, and she kept her arms too stiff to allow him to pull her as close as he obviously wanted to. She was wearing a nearly backless black evening gown, and the sudden remembrance of just how much of her bare skin was showing made her feel self-conscious for the first time. It was difficult enough for her to think clearly when she was near him; if she felt those strong, clever hands touch the highly sensitive skin of her lower back or spine, she was reasonably sure she wouldn't be able to think at all.

Not that she wanted *him* to know that, of course.

"Would you please shed your Don Juan suit and get serious?" she requested.

He chuckled softly, dancing with grace and without effort. "That was the bald truth, sweet."

"Yeah, right." Morgan sighed and couldn't help glancing around somewhat nervously, even though she kept the polite smile pasted to her lips and made sure her voice was low enough to escape being overheard. "Look, there are a dozen private guards watching over Leo Cassady's collection, and at least one cop here as a guest. Surely you aren't thinking—"

"You're the one who isn't thinking, Morgana." His voice was low as well, but casual and unconcerned. "I prefer the secrecy of darkness and the anonymity of a mask, remember? Besides that, it would be rude in the extreme; I would never think of relieving our host of his valuables. No, I am simply here as a guest—an invited guest. Alexander Brandon at your service, ma'am. My friends call me Alex."

As she danced automatically and gazed up at him, Morgan reminded herself of several things. First, *Quinn* was only a nickname, a pseudonym for a faceless thief that had been coined by a British journalist years before. Alexander was certainly his real first name—she believed that much since he'd been practically on his deathbed when he'd admitted it—but since he and Jared Chavalier were brothers, the name of Brandon was undoubtedly no more than a cover for whatever he was up to.

Second, if Quinn was here in Leo Cassady's home by invitation, someone must have vouched for him. Max, perhaps? He was really the only one who could have, she thought. Maxim Bannister was probably the only man Leo would trust enough to admit a stranger to his home.

And, third, Morgan reminded herself of just how tangled this entire situation had become. The Mysteries Past exhibit would open to the public tomorrow, on Friday. Max, and Jared—who was a cop with Interpol—were using the exhibit of the Bannister collection as bait to catch a thief—but not Quinn, because he was working with them. Wolfe Nickerson, a security expert with Lloyd's of London, was officially responsible for the safety of the collection, and Morgan wasn't certain how much *he* knew—though she thought he knew Quinn.

It had gotten to the point where Morgan didn't know how much she could safely say depending on who she was talking to, and she was beginning to feel annoyed about it.

"You dance divinely, Morgana," Quinn said with his usual beguiling charm, smiling down at her. "I knew you would. But if you'd only relax just a bit . . ." His hand exerted a slight pressure at her waist in an attempt to draw her closer.

"No," she said, resisting successfully without losing the rhythm of the dance.

His smile twisted a bit, though his wicked green eyes were alight with amusement. "So reluctant to trust me? I only want to obey the spirit of this dance and hold you closer."

Morgan refused to be seduced. It was almost impossible, but she refused. "Never mind the spirit. You're holding me close enough."

That roguish gaze dropped to examine briefly the low-cut neckline of her black evening gown, and he said wistfully, "Not nearly close enough to suit me."

For her entire adult life—and most of her teens—Morgan had fought almost constantly against the tendency of people, especially men, to assume that her generous bust was undoubtedly matched by an IQ in the low two digits, and so she tended to bristle whenever any man called attention to her measurements either by word or by look.

Any man except Quinn, that is. He had the peculiar knack of saying things that were utterly outrageous and yet made her want to giggle, and she always felt that his interest was as sincerely admiring of nature's generous beauty as it was—almost comically—lustful.

"Well, you'll just have to suffer," she told him in the most severe tone she could manage.

He sighed. "I've been suffering since the night we met, Morgana."

She didn't bother to point out that on two separate occasions, she had quite bluntly invited him to be her lover; he was in one of his verbal fencing moods and wouldn't take her seriously, she knew. Aside from which, she wasn't willing to remind him of his rejection.

"Tough," she muttered.

"You're a hard woman. I've said that before, haven't I?"

He'd been wearing a towel and a bandage at the time. Morgan shoved the memory away. "Look, I just want to know what you're doing here. And *don't* say dancing with me."

"All right, I won't," he said affably. "What I'm doing here is attending a party."

Morgan gritted her teeth, but kept smiling. "I'm in no mood to fence with you. Did Max get you into the house?"

"I've been on the guest list for this party since the beginning, sweet."

Forgetting to keep smiling, she frowned up at him. "What? You couldn't have been. Leo's always planned to throw a party the night before the Mysteries Past opening, and he sent out invitations more than a month ago—in fact, nearly two months ago. How could you possibly—"

Quinn shook his head slightly, then guided her away from the center of the room. Not many of the guests seemed to take note of them, but Morgan caught a glimpse of Max Bannister watching from the other side of the room, his gray eyes unreadable.

Now that she knew Quinn was—at least at the moment—helping Interpol catch another thief, Morgan didn't feel quite so troubled about her previous encounters with the cat burglar, and after having nursed him back to health when he'd been shot weeks ago, she could hardly look on him as a stranger. But she also knew that their relationship—for want of a better term—was yet another complication in an already knotty situation surrounding the Mysteries Past exhibit.

Max had every right to be upset with her, she thought. And he probably was, even though he'd said nothing to make her think so. Still, he was paying her to direct his exhibit, not to socialize with a cat burglar.

Aside from which, she really had no business consorting with a known criminal.

Strange how she kept forgetting that's what Quinn *was*.

He led her from the crowded ballroom without giving her a chance to protest, finding his way easily down a short hallway and out onto a slightly chilly, deserted terrace. Leo hadn't opened the French doors of the ballroom, probably because it had been raining when the party began; the flagstone terrace was still wet, and a heavy fog was creeping in over the garden. Still, if a guest *did* happen to wander out, the party's host was prepared: there were Japanese-type lanterns hung to provide light for the terrace and garden, along with scattered tables and chairs, which were very wet at the moment.

Everything gleamed from the rain, and the incoming fog made the garden an eerie sight. It was very quiet on the terrace, unnaturally so, with the thick mist providing its usual muffling effect; both the music from the ballroom and the sounds of the ocean could only just be heard.

Morgan assumed that Quinn wanted to talk to her without the greater chance of being overheard inside, so she made no effort to protest or to ask him why he'd brought her out here.

Still holding one of her hands, Quinn half sat on the stone balustrade edging the terrace and laughed softly as if some private joke amused him greatly. "Tell me something, Morgana. Have you ever stopped to think that I might be . . . more than Quinn?"

"What do you mean?"

His wide, powerful shoulders lifted in a shrug, and those vivid eyes remained on her face. "Well, Quinn is a creature of the night. His name's a cover, a nickname–"

"An alias," she supplied helpfully.

He let out a low laugh. "All right, an alias. My point is that he moves in the shadows, his face masked to the world—most of the world, anyway—and few know very much about him. But it isn't always night, Morgana. Masks tend to look a bit peculiar in the daylight, and Quinn would hardly have a passport or driver's license—to say nothing of a dinner jacket. So who do you think I am when I'm not Quinn?"

Oddly enough, that question hadn't even occurred to Morgan. "You're . . . Alex," she answered a bit helplessly.

"Yes, but who is Alex?"

"How could I know that?"

"How could you, indeed. After all, Alex Brandon only arrived here yesterday. From England. I'm a collector."

The sheer audacity of him had the usual effect on Morgan; she didn't know whether to laugh or hit him with something. So Alexander Brandon was supposed to be a collector? "Tell me you're kidding," she begged.

He laughed again, the sound still soft. "Afraid not. My daytime persona, you see, is quite well established. Alexander Brandon has a rather nice house in London, which was left to him by his father, as well as apartments in Paris and New York. He has dual citizenship—British and American. He manages a number of investments, also inherited, so he doesn't really have to work unless he wants to. And he seldom wants to. However, he travels quite a bit. And he collects gems."

Morgan had the feeling her mouth was hanging open.

With a smothered sound that might have been another laugh, Quinn went on carelessly. "His family name is quite well respected. So well, in fact, that you might find it on most any list of socially and financially powerful families—on either side of the Atlantic. And Leo Cassady sent him an invitation to this party nearly two months ago—which he accepted."

"Of all the gall," Morgan said wonderingly.

Knowing she wasn't talking about Leo, Quinn sighed mournfully. "Yes, I know. I'm beyond redemption."

Frowning at him, she said, "Is that how Max knows you? From this blameless other life you created for yourself, I mean? And Wolfe?"

"We have encountered one another a few times over the years. Though neither of them knew I was Quinn until fairly recently," Quinn murmured.

"That must have been a shock for them," she said.

"Yes."

Morgan was still frowning. "So . . . now you're openly here in San Francisco, as Alexander Brandon, scion of a noble family and well known as a collector of rare and precious gems."

"Exactly."

"Where are you staying?"

"I have a suite at the Imperial."

It was one of the newer and more luxurious hotels to grace Nob Hill, a fact that shouldn't have surprised Morgan. If Quinn was playing the part of a rich collector, then he'd naturally stay at the best hotel in town. But she couldn't help wondering . . .

"Is Interpol paying the bills?" she asked bluntly.

"No. I am."

"You are? Wait a minute now. You're spending your own money, quite probably ill-gotten gains, to maintain this cover of yours so that you can help Interpol catch a thief so they won't put you in prison?"

Quinn tugged at her hand slightly so that she took a step closer to him; she was standing almost between his knees. "You put things so colorfully—but, yes, that's the gist of it. I don't know why that should surprise you, Morgana."

"Well, it does." She brooded over the question, hardly aware of their closeness. "It's an awfully elaborate situation for someone who's supposedly just trying to keep his tail out of prison. Unless . . . Has this other thief done something to you? You personally?"

Quinn's voice was dry. "Aside from putting a bullet in me, you mean?"

Morgan had a flash of memory: Quinn lying in her bed unconscious, that awful wound high on his chest, and something inside her tightened in remembered pain. With an effort, she managed to push the memory away. It reminded her, though, that here was another question she should have asked—and *hadn't* simply because she'd been so preoccupied with the vexing reality of Quinn's effect on her.

"He's the one who shot you? Is that why you're doing this? Because he shot you?"

Quinn was holding her hand against his thigh, and looked down at it for a moment before he met her eyes. In the soft glow of the lanterns, the light diffused by the mist curling around them, he looked unusually serious. "That would be reason enough for most people."

"What else?"

"Does there have to be another reason?"

Morgan nodded. "For you? Yes, I think so. You've tried your best to convince me you're out for nobody except Quinn—but I'm having a hard time believing that. If you're as selfish and self-involved as you say, why not just go through the motions to satisfy Interpol? Why put yourself—and your own money—on the line if you don't have to?"

"Who says I don't have to? Interpol can be a harsh taskmaster, sweet."

"Maybe so, but I have a feeling you have better motives than just saving your own skin."

"Don't paint me with noble colors, Morgana," he said softly. "In the first storm, they'll wash off. And you'll be disappointed at what's underneath."

It held echoes of something he'd tried to tell her before, a warning not to get involved with him on an intimate level, and though Morgan appreciated the spirit of the warning, she was determined not to allow him to hold her off—even to save herself heartache.

He was a criminal, yes. He had, as his own brother had said bitterly, looted Europe for the better part of ten years. And he was on the side of the angels now only because the choice was preferable to going to prison.

She *knew* that, all of it. But from the night they had met weeks ago—nine weeks and three days ago, to be precise—she had been fighting a losing battle with her common sense.

If only he wasn't so damned intriguing, she thought ruefully. But he was. An outlaw with charm. A green-eyed devil who could steal a necklace right off her neck, later enrage her with the mocking gift of a concubine ring, and yet turn up on her doorstep wounded and vulnerable, trusting her with his life. He was quick-witted and highly intelligent, humorous and curiously well mannered—if that could be said about a thief.

He had . . . *style*. It was something Morgan had never encountered in any man she'd ever met before him, and it was unexpectedly seductive.

"Morgana?"

She blinked, realizing only then that her silence had spanned several minutes. "Hmm?"

"Did you hear what I said?"

Morgan found herself smiling a little, because he sounded so aggrieved. "Yes, I heard what you said."

"And?"

"And—I'm not painting you with noble colors. Or gilding you, for that matter. I just happen to believe you aren't after this other thief only because he shot you, or only because Interpol thinks you're the ace up their sleeve." She eyed him thoughtfully. "Just who is this other thief? I keep forgetting to ask."

He paused, this time for several minutes, and when he finally did speak, his voice was unusually flat and clipped. "Interpol calls him Nightshade. He's been active about eight years—maybe more, but that long at least. Mostly here in the States, a few times in Europe. He's very, very good. And he kills anybody who gets in his way."

Morgan didn't realize she had shivered until Quinn released her hand to take his jacket off and drape it around her shoulders. She didn't protest, but said softly, "It isn't that cold out here. But the way you sounded . . ."

His hands remained on her shoulders, long fingers flexing just a bit. "You'll have to forgive me, Morgana. I don't care too much for murderers."

Enveloped in the warmth of his jacket, surrounded by the familiar scent of him, and very aware of his touch, Morgan struggled to keep her attention on the conversation. "Especially when one of them shoots you?"

"Especially then."

She shook her head a little, baffled and intrigued by a man who could cheerfully admit to having been the world's most infamous thief for a decade, and yet spoke of another thief's penchant for violence with chilling loathing in his voice. No wonder she couldn't convince herself Quinn was an evil man; how could she, when his own words had, more than once, shown him to possess very definite principles—even if she hadn't quite figured out what they were.

"Who are you, Alex?" she asked quietly.

His hands tightened on her shoulders, drawing her a step closer, and his sensual mouth curved in a slight, curiously self-mocking smile. "I'm Quinn. No matter who else, or what else, I'm Quinn. Never forget that, Morgana."

She watched her hands lift to his broad chest, her fingers probing to feel him through the crisp white shirt. They were very close, so close she felt enveloped by him, and even though a wise little voice in her head reminded her sternly that he had twice rejected her— for whatever reason—she couldn't seem to make herself draw away from him.

He had kissed her before, once as a teasing ploy to distract her so that he could filch her necklace, and again in the hulk of an abandoned building when they had narrowly escaped with their lives. After that, even during the days and nights he'd spent in her apartment recovering from a wound, he had been careful not to allow desire to spark into something more between them, and when she'd thrown caution to the winds, he had simply left, removing himself and the problem of his response to her.

Morgan might have been devastated, all things considered, but she'd had a feeling he would come to her again. And he had. Ostensibly to thank her for her care while he was healing, but really, she thought, because he'd wanted to see her. Because he couldn't help pushing, as he'd once told her himself, couldn't help walking the fine line dividing what it was possible for him to get away with—and what wasn't.

Because he wanted what he'd convinced himself he could never have.

She thought he honestly believed he would be bad for her, and that was why he turned mocking or reminded her of just who and what he was whenever she got too close. And he was probably right, she told herself fiercely. He would no doubt be *very* bad for her, and she'd have only herself to blame if she was crazy enough to let herself fall for a thief.

But knowing that did nothing to prevent her from melting against him when he pulled her suddenly into his arms, and it didn't stop her from lifting her face invitingly. When his hard, warm mouth closed over hers, she gave a little purr of guileless pleasure and responded instantly.

Quinn hadn't planned on this when he had brought Morgan out here to talk—but then, his plans never seemed to turn out the way he'd intended when she was around. She had the knack of making him forget all his good intentions.

The road to hell is paved with good intentions.

An apt proverb, he thought, and then he forgot to think at all, because he could feel her hips between his thighs and her splendid breasts pressed against his chest, and her soft mouth was eager under his. The smooth material of his jacket covered her back and shoulders, denying him access to bare flesh, but he imagined a silky warmth and that was enough to send him to the very edge of his control.

One of his hands slid up her back to her nape, bared by her elegant hairstyle, and he cupped her head to hold it steady as if she might try to escape him. But she didn't try. Her mouth opened beneath the insistent pressure of his, accepting the small possession of his tongue, and her tremor of response was echoed by a shudder of desire deep in his own body.

Quinn wanted more, a lot more, and if there'd been a bed—hell, even a thin rug—nearby, he very likely would have forgotten everything else except the woman in his arms. But there was no bed or rug, just a wet, foggy terrace outside a ballroom where a party was in full swing, and where he was supposed to be looking for a ruthless thief—

"Excuse me." The voice was brusque rather than apologetic, and too determined to ignore.

Quinn lifted his head slowly, gazing down at Morgan's sleepy eyes and dazed expression, and if he hadn't been related by blood to the man who'd interrupted them, he probably would have committed a very satisfying murder.

"Go away, Jared," he said, his rough voice not yet under control.

"No," Jared replied with wonderful simplicity. He stood as if rooted to the terrace.

Quinn said something very rude, which didn't budge his brother but did make Morgan recall her surroundings. She pushed herself back away from him, blinking, absolutely appalled to realize that she had totally forgotten the presence of a hundred people partying just yards away.

Her only solace was the knowledge that Quinn had been as involved as she, unlikely to have rejected her *this* time—but that was little comfort.

"I—I'll just go back inside," she murmured, startled by the husky sound of her voice. "Oh—your jacket." She swung the dinner jacket from around her shoulders and handed it to Quinn, then more or less fled into the house.

He didn't follow her.

Morgan automatically began to make her way back to the ballroom, but she was met in the short hallway by a petite blonde with fierce green eyes who immediately took her arm and led her toward the powder room instead.

"A bit damp out, I guess," Storm Tremaine drawled.

"It's stopped raining," Morgan said, experimenting with her voice and relieved to find it nearly normal.

"Really? I never would have known."

Morgan was baffled by that lazy comment until she got a look at herself in the powder-room mirror. "Oh, God," she moaned.

"Yeah, I thought you might like to pull yourself together before the cream of San Francisco society got an eyeful," Storm said, sitting down in a boudoir chair before the tile vanity while her friend claimed the other chair. They were, thankfully, alone in the spacious room. "Where's your purse?"

"I don't know. I think it was on that little table just inside the ballroom. I think." Morgan was attempting to tuck unruly strands of her long black hair back into its former elegant style, unsure if it had been the dampness outside or Quinn's fingers that had wrought such damage.

"Here, then." Storm handed over a small hairbrush and several pins. "Your makeup looks okay. Except for—"

"I know," Morgan muttered, all too aware that her lipstick was a bit smeared. Nobody looking at her could doubt she had just been thoroughly kissed.

Propping an elbow on the vanity as she watched her friend, Storm said, "Quinn?"

"How did you know who he was? I mean—" Morgan stopped herself with a sigh as she realized. "Wolfe, of course." Since Storm was engaged to Wolfe Nickerson, there were likely few secrets between them.

"Of course. He introduced us just before you got

waltzed out onto the terrace. So your Quinn is Alexander Brandon, huh?"

"So he says." Having done what she could with her hair, Morgan used a tissue and Storm's lipstick to repair the rest of the damage to her pride.

"And he's gone public, so to speak. It's an interesting ploy, I admit, especially if he's so sure the thief he's after also wears a blameless public face."

Morgan returned the lipstick and, very carefully, said, "Tell me something, friend. Is there anybody who *doesn't* know what Quinn's up to?"

"Outside our own little circle, I certainly hope so." Storm smiled slightly. "Wolfe said you'd probably hit me with something when I told you just how much I do know, but I'm counting on your sweet disposition."

"Oh, yeah? I wouldn't count on that if I were you. I'm not in a real good mood right now."

Solemnly, Storm said, "Then I'll have to risk your wrath, I suppose."

"Just spit it out, will you?"

"I don't really work for Ace Security," Storm told her in that solemn voice. "I'm with Interpol."

Morgan didn't have to look in the mirror to know her mouth had fallen open in shock. "Interpol? Like Jared?"

"Uh-huh. He's more or less my boss, at least on this assignment. I hope this room isn't bugged," she added thoughtfully, glancing around.

"Why would it be bugged?"

"No reason I can think of." Apologetically, Storm added, "They teach us to be paranoid."

Morgan was torn between fascination and irritation: fascination because her rather ordinary world had grown in the last two months to include internationally famous cat burglars and Interpol agents, and irritated because those around her had taken their own sweet time letting her in on their plans.

Amused, Storm said, "Don't blow up, now. If it makes you feel any better, I didn't know Quinn was in on this until just the other day, and I had no idea that all the guys knew him."

Suddenly curious, Morgan said, "Quinn told me that Max and Wolfe didn't know about his burgling until recently. Did Wolfe tell you how he found out?"

"Umm. Caught him with his hand in a safe in London about a year ago."

Morgan winced. "That must have been quite an encounter."

"The word Wolfe used was 'tense.'"

"I can imagine." Morgan sighed. "I wonder how Max found out."

"No idea. And Jared's so furious on the subject I haven't dared ask him. Can't really blame him, I suppose. Nice thing, for an international cop to find out his own brother's an international thief. A bit awkward."

"To say the least," Morgan murmured, remembering how Jared had told her not to "get any fool ideas about nobility" into her head concerning Quinn's current association with Interpol.

"A bit awkward for you too," Storm said quietly.

Awkward? Morgan considered the word and found that her friend had picked a good one.

As the director of an utterly priceless collection of gems and artworks about to go on public display, Morgan had access to something that any thief would have sold more than his soul to possess. Any thief.

It was easy enough to say the collection was safe from Quinn, that he was walking the straight and narrow now, bound to help catch a thief he clearly despised. Easy enough to let his charm sway her, his desire ignite hers. Easy enough to gaze into his beguiling green eyes and convince herself that she saw something in him the world would find surprising—if not downright inconceivable.

Easy enough to tell herself she wasn't a fool.

Morgan looked at her reflection in the mirror, seeing a woman who was once again elegant, but whose lips still bore the faintly smudged appearance of having been kissed with hungry passion.

"Awkward," she said. "Yes, you could say that."

TWO

"Did anybody ever tell you your timing is lousy?" Quinn asked, shrugging into his jacket. His voice was back to normal, light and rather careless.

"Only you," Jared replied. "But I could say the same thing about your timing. Alex, there are a hundred people in that house, and if your theory is correct, one of them is Nightshade. So what the hell are you doing necking on the terrace?"

"We weren't necking," Quinn replied somewhat indignantly. "We hadn't gotten that far—thanks to you."

Jared let out a short laugh, but he didn't sound very amused. "For once in your life will you get serious?"

"I'm completely serious." Quinn stood up and smoothed his jacket, buttoning it neatly. When he spoke again, his voice was more sober. "I had to talk to Morgan. This is the first time she's seen me socially, and if I hadn't told her who I was supposed to be, God only knows what might have happened. She tends to be a bit impulsive."

"I know," Jared said dryly.

Quinn shrugged. "So, since I had no idea how she'd react, it seemed more prudent to bring her out here."

Jared didn't bother to point out that they hadn't been talking very much when he'd interrupted them. "Well, do you think you could put your love life on hold long enough to get some work done? You can't really study all the guests if you're out here on the terrace."

"The night is young," Quinn reminded him lightly.

Jared knew only too well that he had about as much hope of controlling Quinn as any man had in controlling the wind, but that didn't stop him from trying. "You aren't planning on doing a little night hunting after the party, are you?"

"That depends on what I find here."

"Alex, it's too risky for you to play both parts all the time and you know it." Jared's voice had roughened.

Quinn's voice remained light. "I know my limits— and the risks. I also have burned in my mind that one good glimpse I got of Nightshade just before he shot me, and if I see anyone tonight who even *seems* to move the same way he did, I won't let him out of my sight."

Jared didn't speak immediately, and when he did, it was to make a serious comment. "We did have a few women on the list; if you're so sure Nightshade's a man, at least that narrows the possibilities."

"I'm sure, though I couldn't tell you exactly why. The way he moved, or something else. Hell, maybe I caught a whiff of after-shave just before he fired. Anyway, all I can do for the moment is look for anything familiar and listen in case the bastard gives himself away somehow."

"The chances of that have to be slim to none."

"Think positive," Quinn advised. "It's always worked for me. Now, don't you think we'd better return to the party before the wrong person notices something odd?"

Jared waited until Quinn took several steps away from him before saying, "Alex?"

Quinn half turned to look back at him. "Yeah?"

"That's a snappy shade of lipstick you're wearing. Better suited to a brunette, though."

With a low laugh, Quinn produced a snowy-white handkerchief and removed the evidence of his interlude with Morgan. Then he half saluted Jared and went back into the house.

Jared waited for several minutes just so they wouldn't reappear inside at the same time. And if anyone had been on the damp, chilly terrace to hear him speak, they might have been surprised at what he muttered to himself.

"I wonder when all this is going to blow up in my face."

⊰❈⊱―――――⊰❈⊱

Morgan caught glimpses of Quinn throughout the next couple of hours, but she took care to keep herself too busy to watch him. Since she never lacked for dancing partners and was well known to most of the guests, it was easy enough to look and act as if she were enjoying the party and had nothing more serious on her mind than who to dance with next or whether or not she wanted to try a champagne cocktail.

The appearance was, to say the least, deceptive. Morgan did quite a lot of thinking while she danced and smiled. Ever since she had faced up to a few unnerving things in the powder room, she had been thinking more seriously than she could ever remember doing in her life.

It occurred to her at some point during the evening that the interlude with Quinn out on the terrace might have more than one explanation. Yes, he had wanted to talk to her privately, no doubt because he had to make certain she understood why he'd suddenly appeared in public. But there might have been another motive in his agile mind.

As a collector, he could be expected to visit the Mysteries Past exhibit, but it would certainly look a bit odd if he began haunting the museum—something he probably wanted to do in order to remain close to the trap's bait. However, if he made it obvious that he was drawn to the museum by something other than the lure of the Bannister collection—her, for instance—then no one would be very surprised to find him there.

Morgan didn't want to accept that possibility, but it fit too logically to be denied. After all, prior to this evening, Quinn had quite definitely said he wouldn't be her lover—whether in an honest effort to protect her from whatever pain he might cause her or simply and more selfishly to save himself from having to deal with an unwanted and unnecessary problem. Twice they had been completely alone together in her apartment when she had all but thrown herself at him, and twice he had walked away without even kissing her.

Why, then, had he chosen a damp, foggy terrace in the middle of a party to suddenly change his mind? Because he'd been overwhelmed by desire? Hardly, Morgan thought reluctantly. He had wanted her, yes; she was sure of that. He had been more than a little annoyed when Jared interrupted them.

But . . . In a way, he'd been safe in starting something when and where he had. No matter how passionate the interlude had become, it was highly unlikely that they would have made love out there—the surroundings had been too cold, far too wet, and hideously uncomfortable, as well as lacking in privacy.

He was an intelligent man, and Morgan doubted that he was often taken by surprise; nearly a decade of eluding the police forces of the world made that fairly obvious. So it seemed clear he would have had the foresight to know nothing irrevocable would happen between them on the terrace.

Morgan told herself that it was just speculation, there was no proof he meant to make her a part of his cover—but when he cut in neatly to take her away from the gallery owner she'd been dancing with, her suspicions grew. And they grew even more when he managed to hold her far closer than she had allowed during their first dance, so that her hands were on his shoulders and his were on her back.

"You've been ignoring me, Morgana," he reproved, smiling down at her.

He was an intriguing, charming, conniving *scoundrel*, Morgan decided with a building anger that was welcome. Worse, he was a heartless thief who would steal a necklace right off a woman's neck while he kissed her—and if there was anything lower than that, she didn't know what it could be.

The anger felt so good that Morgan wrapped herself with it, and it was such strong armor she was able to return his smile with perfect ease, undisturbed by their closeness or by the touch of his warm hands on her bare back. "Well, since I haven't been told how well I'm supposed to know you, I thought it best. We *have* just met tonight, right?"

"Yes—but it must have been love at first sight," he said soulfully.

"Oh, I see." Morgan allowed her arms to slip up around his neck, turning the dance into something far more intimate than even he had intended. She veiled her eyes with her lashes, fixing them on his neat tie, and made her smile seductive. "You should have told me."

She thought her voice was seductive as well, but there must have been something there to give her away, because Quinn didn't buy the act.

He was silent for a moment or so while they danced, then cleared his throat and said in a matter-of-fact voice, "You're mad as hell, aren't you?"

Her lashes lifted as she met his wary eyes, and she knew her own were probably, as he'd once observed, spitting rage just like a cat's. In a silken tone, she said, "I passed mad as hell about an hour ago. You don't want to know what I am now."

"I'm rather glad you aren't armed, I know that much," he murmured.

She let him feel several long fingernails gently caress the sensitive nape of his neck. "Don't be too sure."

"I've said it before, I know, but you look magnificent when you're angry, Morgana." He gave her a smile, this one seemingly genuine, amused—and a bit sheepish. And his deep voice was unusually sincere when he went on. "If you like, I'll stop right here in front of God and San Francisco and apologize on bended knee. I'm a cad and a louse, and I should have asked for your help instead of trying to use you. I'm sorry."

It was a totally disarming apology, and Morgan wasn't surprised to feel her rage begin to drain away. Irritably, she said, "Well, why didn't you?"

"I thought you'd say no," he replied simply.

Since she was as quick-witted as he was, it took only a moment for Morgan to understand his reasoning. She

didn't speak immediately, because the music stopped
and Quinn led her out of the ballroom a second time.
Instead of returning to the terrace, however, he took
her arm and guided her through the mansion into one
of the first-floor rooms—this one a spacious parlor—
where Leo Cassady displayed part of his valuable collection of artworks. The room was open to guests, but
was currently deserted except for them.

They were far enough from the door that they
weren't likely to be overheard by anyone outside the
room. Still, Morgan kept her voice quiet. "You mean
you thought I wouldn't want to pretend we were involved because . . ."

"Because I was a jerk and walked out on you twice,"
he finished, giving her a very direct look.

He was being very disarming—but Morgan wasn't
completely disarmed. She pulled gently from his grasp
and half turned to face him, paying no attention to the
priceless oil painting hanging on the wall beside them.
"Uh-huh. So you figured you'd just sweep me off my
feet and do enough romancing to convince whoever
happened to be watching that you'd fallen for me? As
an excuse to hang around the museum?"

Quinn hesitated, a considering look in his brilliant
green eyes. Then he sighed. "Something like that. But
my motives weren't entirely selfish, I swear."

"Oh, no?"

He hesitated again, then swore under his breath.
"All right, they are. But not the way you think."

"Then explain it to me," she requested.

Smiling suddenly, his voice wry, he said, "I must be out of my mind. Morgana, the simple truth is that I can't stay away from you. I'm sure you've noticed that much. Even though my better self tells me I have no right to get involved with you, I can't seem to listen. I keep coming back, finding excuses—even lousy ones— to be with you."

She wanted to believe him, but Morgan wasn't willing to cave in so easily. "The simple truth, Alex? Maybe. But I'm sure you'll forgive me if I reserve judgment on that. As I recall, you once told me yourself I was wise to believe you couldn't be trusted. I can't see that anything's changed since then."

"I was masked then," he said. "I'm not now."

Morgan had the odd feeling he didn't mean just a black ski mask, but something else, something much less easy to define. As if he felt himself to be vulnerable with her, somehow unguarded or unprotected. She studied his face, looking for something that would tell her if she could trust him.

His face had been imprinted in her mind from the first time she'd seen it. A face that was lean and very handsome, with high cheekbones and a strong jaw. His eyes were startling, a rare pale shade of green, surrounded by ridiculously long lashes, and very vivid and expressive. Brows that slanted a bit, and a mouth that was curved with humor and sensuality.

If he'd been dark, Morgan thought vaguely, brooding or sardonic, it might have been easier to believe the worst of him. But he was fair and handsome, even his voice was beautiful, and how was a woman supposed to *know*?

"Damn you," she murmured.

His face softened. "That's one reason I kept walking away from you, whether you believe it or not. You don't trust me, and without trust between lovers, it always ends in regret. Oh, you're attracted—we're both attracted. And for some women, that would be enough. But not for you. I knew that the night you followed a gang of thugs into an abandoned building to help me."

That had been the first time she'd seen his face, she remembered. And it had been the night he had said he thought she would break his heart.

"I want to trust you," she said slowly. "But every time I think I can, something happens to make me wonder."

"It isn't that I'm Quinn; we both know that. This is something else. Something deeper, more basic."

She nodded silently. Though she hadn't yet come to terms with her feelings about that part of him, it wasn't what troubled her now. This wasn't a matter of trusting a thief, it was a matter of trusting a man.

His wide shoulders lifted in a faint shrug. "What am I supposed to do—preface every remark by saying this is the truth? I can't even do that, Morgana. So much of what I have to do here is pretense, living a role, playing a part—and sometimes I have to lie to everyone."

"Then what am *I* supposed to do?" she asked. "You

as good as tell me you've lied to me, *will* lie to me—how do I know anything you're saying now is the truth?"

"You don't," he said softly.

Morgan began to turn away, but Quinn caught her hand and held her in place, not forcefully but firmly.

"I wish there was something else I could say, but there isn't. I know how unfair I'm being in asking you to try and trust me when I've given you no reason—except one."

"What reason?" she demanded.

"I trusted you."

Staring up into green eyes that seemed painfully honest, she knew it was true. He had trusted her. He had trusted her with his life, coming to her after he'd been shot. He had trusted her with his freedom, trusted her not to call the police or the newspapers when she might have, when she hadn't known he was working with Interpol.

It made most of the fight drain out of her. "So where does that leave us?" she asked.

"That's up to you," he replied, his voice still quiet. "We're both involved with the exhibit, but we don't have to be involved with each other."

"You need a reason to hang around the museum," she heard herself say.

Quinn smiled slightly. "That was the easiest plan, but not the only one. Besides, I doubt very much if anyone would dare try to steal the collection in broad daylight while the museum is open to the public and filled with people. It'll happen at night. And at night, I'm Quinn."

He was still holding her hand, and she looked down at his with a curious sense of being poised on the brink of something. His was a skilled hand, she thought, even if the skills were nefarious. A strong hand. He had saved her life at least once and probably twice—how could she not trust him?

She returned her gaze to his face, and spoke carefully. "Can you answer one question—and swear to me it's the truth?"

His smile went a bit crooked. "I'll have to hear it first."

She had expected that much. "You said you couldn't seem to stay away from me. Whatever you feel about me, does it have anything—anything at all—to do with the collection?"

Quinn instantly shook his head. "No—I swear. And I'll swear to something else, Morgana. I'll swear to you right now that I will never again try to use you or whatever is between us for my own ends."

Morgan found herself smiling. "I ought to have my head examined for believing you." To her surprise, he lifted her hand briefly to his lips.

"Thank you for that," he said.

The unexpected caress made her suddenly aware of her heartbeat, but she tried to keep her voice steady. "So, does this mean we are going to get involved?"

Quinn carried her hand to the crook of his arm and

started for the door. "It's getting late. Why don't I take you home."

"Answer me, Alex," she insisted.

He paused to look down at her with very bright eyes and said, "We've been involved since the night we met. The only difference is that now we both know it—and admit it. And the only question is how long it's going to take me to convince you to trust me."

Morgan didn't know whether to feel moved by his apparent determination or frustrated. "I gather trust is a prerequisite for taking the next logical step in our involvement?"

"Certainly. I told you what happens when there's no trust between lovers. Regrets. No matter what happens between us, sweet, you aren't going to regret me. Not if I have anything to say about it."

He was slipping into his Don Juan persona, but Morgan didn't protest. She had the feeling that both of them had taken all the emotional probing they could stand for one night. Besides that, she enjoyed Quinn in all his personas—even when they maddened her.

Walking obediently beside him as he headed for the front of the house, she said, "Unless it's after midnight, we'll be the first guests to leave. Leo's parties are famous for lasting into the wee hours."

"It's just after eleven," he said.

Morgan looked up at him curiously. "You aren't wearing a watch, and I haven't seen a clock. How do you . . ."

"One of my many talents. I have a very accurate

clock in my head, seldom off by more than five minutes."

"That must come in handy. You want to list your other talents? Just so I won't miss any of them?"

Quinn chuckled. "I'll let you discover them one by one. It's much more fun that way."

It didn't take long for them to collect their coats and say their thanks to their host—though Morgan had to bite down on the inside of her cheek to keep from laughing at Leo's well-bred surprise at their haste.

In a confiding tone to his host, Quinn said, "I want to get her completely alone so I can propose."

"Fast work, Alex," Leo noted mildly. "Should I congratulate you?"

"No," Morgan said, rather surprised to find herself playing along willingly. "Leo, can I trust this man to take me home? Are you sure he isn't an escaped lunatic or something? He's acting very strangely."

"He's a collector," Leo said soothingly. "All of us are odd, Morgan, you know that."

"Yes, but is he dangerous?"

"I shouldn't think so. I bought a painting from him about three years ago in London, and he seemed perfectly all right then."

Morgan didn't dare look up at Quinn. Of all the gall! she thought, torn between amusement and horror. Had he sold poor Leo a stolen painting?

"I am not dangerous to life and limb," Quinn said virtuously, "but only to the heart. I fell in love with her cat's eyes, Leo. Say good night, Morgana."

With a long-suffering sigh, she said, "Good night, Leo."

Leo's eyes were twinkling. "Good night, Morgan. I'll probably see you tomorrow at the opening." He had, of course, attended the private showing the previous Saturday but, like many collectors, wanted another look at the Bannister collection.

Morgan found herself swept out the front door and installed in the front seat of a low-slung sports car with a European pedigree. She waited until the engine roared to life and the powerful little car had left Leo's house far behind before she spoke to her companion.

"Is that how you met Leo? The painting?"

"That's how," he answered cheerfully.

"You've got a lot of nerve," she said. "Was it a stolen painting?"

Quinn made a little "tsk" sound and said, "I believe I'll plead the Fifth on that question."

It was what she had expected. Sighing, she said, "Well, at least things are getting clearer to me. I knew Max was introducing Jared as a friend and private security expert, which nobody would be surprised by, and I knew Wolfe's position as Lloyd's security expert was out in the open, but when I saw you there tonight, all I could think was that one of us had lost our mind."

"Still a possibility," Quinn reminded her lightly.

She looked at his profile, which was visible to her only occasionally in the lights of the street lamps and passing cars. Ignoring his comment, she said, "It makes sense, though, that you've had to have a daytime persona all these years, and that there would be people who know you only as Alex Brandon. But I still say it was crazy for you to be a collector by day and a cat burglar by night. Is crazy, I mean."

"Actually, it makes perfect sense," he told her.

"Only to a lunatic."

"I'll try not to take that personally."

Morgan had to laugh, and shook her head a bit bemusedly. "I've called you worse things, believe me. You should have heard me when I got the concubine ring."

It was Quinn's turn to laugh. "I suppose I should say I'm sorry about that, Morgana, but I'd be lying. I happened to have that copy with me, and I just couldn't resist. I knew you'd recognize it, of course, and I knew you'd be furious." He hesitated, then said, "You didn't mention it when I was staying at your place."

"I also didn't ask who shot you—or a few other logical questions I should have asked. You seem to have a peculiar effect on my mind."

"That's the nicest thing you've ever said to me."

She knew she should have replied to that lightly to keep the conversation easygoing, but her own words had reminded her of just how much danger Quinn was probably in.

Since she had first met him *as* Quinn, she had very quickly realized that the newspaper accounts of his daring and nervelessness had not been overstated. He was, she thought, a man who would always react to danger with either cool composure or careless humor—

whichever he judged best suited the situation and increased his chances of success.

But even when there was a question of his very survival, Quinn would never be ruled by fears or uncertainties, and once he made up his mind to do something, not even a bullet would cause him to change course. It might have been determination or just plain stubbornness, but whatever it was made him an ideal man to live any kind of tricky or difficult life.

That was easy to see. It was also clear to Morgan that Quinn enjoyed his life, thrived on it even, and was unlikely to change. If Interpol did indeed decide he was more valuable working for them than languishing in prison, he would no doubt go on living a dangerous double life.

What she didn't know was how she felt about that.

Morgan was an impulsive woman by nature, and occasionally reckless, but she was a long way from fearless. If she ever deliberately put herself in a dangerous situation—as she had when she'd followed that gang of thugs to help Quinn—it would always be because she followed her heart and her instincts, not the cool reason and sharp intelligence that was also hers. And she was one of those people who shone in a crisis, only to quietly fall apart later, when there was time.

"Morgana? You're very quiet."

A little startled, she realized that they had nearly reached her apartment building. "Sorry."

"Is anything wrong?" he asked quietly.

She started to lie and say nothing, but something in

her rebelled. "Wrong? I don't know. I was just thinking about what you're doing. All of you, I guess. Max is risking his collection. Wolfe is risking his job. Jared wears a gun most of the time. And you were shot not so long ago."

"I was careless," Quinn said in a casual tone, treating the matter offhandedly, as if it didn't matter. "And I never make the same mistake twice."

"So I shouldn't worry? Nice try, but I got an unpleasantly good look at what a bullet can do to somebody standing on the wrong end of the gun."

Quinn was silent for a moment, then spoke in a more serious tone. "Everything we do in life carries risk, you know that."

"Yeah, but most of us don't go out looking for trouble."

"Don't we? We drive cars, we fly in airplanes—and some of us even follow dangerous criminals into abandoned buildings."

"I wasn't thinking clearly at the time," she murmured, ruefully aware that he had scored a neat point.

Quinn didn't belabor the point, he just went on calmly. "As one who's taken a few chances in the last ten years, I can tell you it's much better to face a problem head-on, even if it does seem risky."

Morgan decided to abandon the subject for the moment; she had the feeling she wasn't going to score any points. "I just hope you're all going to be careful."

He parked the car in front of Morgan's apartment building and shut off the engine. "That's the plan," he said. He got out of the car and came around to open the door for her.

"Will you be at the museum tomorrow?" she asked him as they walked together into the building and up the stairs to Morgan's third-floor apartment.

"Of course. I'm a collector, remember? And since I arrived in the city after the private showing, I haven't had a chance to see the collection yet."

"Oh, right," Morgan said. "I keep forgetting."

He chuckled as he watched her find her key and unlock the apartment door. "If you forget around the wrong person, we'll all be in trouble."

He didn't sound too worried about it, which pleased Morgan. She'd been told more than once that she talked too much, but Quinn clearly trusted her not to blurt out any of his secrets. The ones she knew, at least.

"I won't," she said, pushing her apartment door open.

"Good. I'll see you tomorrow at the museum."

Morgan felt a pang of disappointment, thinking he was going to leave with no more than a polite good-bye, but before it could take hold of her, Quinn caught her shoulders, bent his head, and covered her mouth with his.

The movement was a bit abrupt, but there was nothing rough about it, and she couldn't have prevented her response no matter what. Her body seemed to have a mind of its own, going boneless and molding itself to his, while her fingers clutched the lapels of his coat helplessly. A curl of heat ignited somewhere deep in her belly, spreading out so rapidly that even her skin felt feverish, and a tremor of pure pleasure rippled through her when she felt his fingers lightly stroke her throat and the nape of her neck. When he finally raised his head, she couldn't help making a little sound of frustration.

Quinn's face was a bit strained, she thought, and his eyes had darkened, but his voice was only slightly husky when he said, "Good night, Morgana."

With a tremendous effort, she managed to let go of his coat and turn away from him. She went into her apartment, where a couple of lamps shed a welcoming light, and closed the door softly. For a long time she leaned back against it, not really thinking, but vaguely bothered by something.

She realized what was different when she reached up to touch her bare throat and found her little ruby necklace there. He had returned it, slipping it into place as deftly as he had removed it weeks before.

THREE

Morgan chided herself for it later, but the truth was that she looked for Quinn at the museum for most of Friday. It wasn't easy considering the crush of people eager to view the Mysteries Past exhibit on this first day of its opening to the public, but she looked for him.

She had even dressed with more care than usual, choosing a slim, calf-length black skirt, a full-sleeved white blouse, and a really beautiful, hand-beaded vest done in opulent gold, black, and hints of rust. The outfit was completed with black pumps, and she wore her long black hair swept up in an elegant French twist.

Morgan had told herself that she had dressed so carefully only because this was the day that Mysteries Past opened, and since she was the director she had a responsibility to look her best . . . but she didn't believe herself. She had dressed with Quinn in mind, and she knew it.

She wanted to look . . . sophisticated and cultured. And tall.

And if it occurred to her that *sexy* might have been added to a description of the appearance she was trying to achieve, she ignored the realization. She looked for Quinn all day, searching the crowd of faces for the one imprinted in her mind. She thought she was being subtle about it, a happy delusion that was shattered when Storm emerged from the computer room somewhere around three in the afternoon.

"You know, I really wouldn't expect to see him here for at least another hour or so," the petite blonde drawled as she joined Morgan near the guards' desk in the museum's lobby. Her little blond cat, Bear, rode her shoulder as usual, so exact a feline replica of Storm that he seemed an eerie familiar.

"See who?" Morgan hugged her clipboard and tried to look innocent. It wasn't her best expression.

Storm pursed her lips slightly, and her green eyes danced. "Alex Brandon."

"Dammit, was I that obvious?"

"Afraid so. The way you keep staring at tall blond men is a little hard to miss. I picked it up on my monitor, as a matter of fact."

Morgan sighed and said dammit again without heat and without self-consciousness. "Well, in that case, why wouldn't you expect to see him for at least another hour?"

Storm glanced casually around to make certain they couldn't be overheard before she replied. "He has to sleep sometime, doesn't he? I imagine he's on watch or on the move most of the night, and since the collection is safest during the day with the museum filled with people, that'd be a good time to sleep."

"I knew that." Morgan frowned at herself.

Storm chuckled. "He probably wasn't in bed before seven or eight this morning, so he likely hasn't been up more than an hour, if that long. I'd give him time for a shave and shower, as well as breakfast, if I were you."

"You've made your point." Morgan sighed. "If this keeps up, I'm never going to see him in the daylight. I mean, he was at my apartment for a couple of days when he was healing, but we didn't go outside, so I haven't actually *seen* him in the sunshine."

"One of your ambitions?"

"Don't laugh, but yes."

"Why on earth would I laugh? It seems a reasonable enough aim to me. Especially if you've the suspicion he's a vampire."

Morgan looked at her friend seriously. "No, because I saw his reflection in a mirror last night at Leo's."

"Oh. Well, that does seem to prove he isn't a creature of the night. Not that kind of creature, anyway. I don't suppose he could be another kind?"

"Only vampires are famous for their seductive but deadly charm," Morgan reminded her, still solemn.

Storm nodded gravely. "That's what I thought. You could wear a cross, I guess, and find out for sure."

Silently, Morgan hooked a finger inside the open

collar of her blouse and held out a fine golden chain from which dangled a polished gold cross. Storm studied the cross, then met Morgan's earnest gaze. Then they both burst out laughing.

A bit unsteadily, Storm said, "Lord, this man must have quite an effect on you if he's got you half-seriously contemplating the undead."

"Let's put it this way. I wouldn't put it past the man to be three parts sorcerer at the very least." Morgan got hold of herself. She looked at her clipboard and tried to remember that she was being paid to do a job. "Umm . . . I have to go do another walk-through of the exhibit and make sure everything's going all right. If anyone should ask—"

"I'll tell him right where you are," Storm assured her.

"If you were a true friend, you'd lash me to the nearest mast before I make an utter fool of myself," Morgan said somewhat mournfully. "All that crafty devil has to do is smile and say something—anything— and I forget all my good intentions."

With a faint smile, Storm said, "I'd be glad to lash you to a mast *if* I thought that was what you really wanted."

"I'm not fooling anybody today, am I?"

"No. But don't let that worry you. We're all entitled to one bit of reckless folly in our lives, Morgan. My daddy taught me that. It's something to remember."

"Have you had yours?" Morgan asked curiously.

The small blonde smiled. "Of course I have. I fell

for Wolfe in the middle of a very tricky situation when I couldn't tell him the truth about myself. It was reckless and foolish—but it turned out all right in the end. Something else for you to remember: often the definition of a foolish act is just . . . bad timing."

Morgan nodded thoughtfully and left her friend, beginning to make her way through the crowded museum toward the Mysteries Past exhibit housed on the second floor and in the west wing of the huge building.

Reckless folly. A good description, Morgan thought. After all, nobody in their right mind would consider this fascination with an internationally notorious cat burglar anything *but* reckless folly. Bad timing? Oh, yes, it was that too.

And knowing all that did absolutely nothing to knock some sense into her normally sensible head, she reflected wryly.

Pushing Quinn out of her thoughts for the moment, Morgan strolled through the exhibit wing, casual but watchful, studying visitor reactions to the various displays as well as noting potential traffic bottlenecks as particular pieces of the Bannister collection drew more interest than others. She jotted several notes to herself, reminders to see about more lighting for one corner, an extra velvet rope to redirect traffic through a particular room, and to have an inconveniently placed bench moved from its present location.

During the remainder of the afternoon, Morgan ruthlessly kept her mind on her job and performed various duties with her usual competence. She answered a few questions from people who knew she was the director of the exhibit—including a number of reporters covering the public opening—returned a few lost children to their parents, and coped with a couple of accidentally triggered alarms (they were still getting the bugs out of the electronic security system).

She also spoke briefly to Max and his wife, Dinah, who paid a fleeting visit to the museum to see how things were going, and to Wolfe, who was around all day but seldom visible as he watched over the collection his employer, Lloyd's of London, insured. She didn't see any sign of Jared, which didn't surprise her; since he and Dani had gotten married the previous Sunday, they had spent most of their time alone together—and who could blame them?

Besides, Jared, like Quinn, would undoubtedly spend more nights than days in the vicinity of the museum since the thief they were intent on luring—Nightshade—was virtually guaranteed to make his move during the dark hours.

Morgan thought about that only fleetingly as the day wore on, partly because she kept herself busy and partly because the deadly danger Nightshade was famous for was something she didn't like to think about. She did her job, and it wasn't until nearly six o'clock, when the museum's visitors were beginning to make their way toward the exits and she was doing a final walk-through of the exhibit for the day, that she saw Quinn.

He was standing alone at the central display case, which held the spectacular Bolling diamond. He was dressed casually in dark slacks and a cream-colored turtleneck sweater, with a black leather jacket worn open. Hands in his pockets, head bent, he stood gazing intently at the priceless seventy-five-carat teardrop canary diamond, and maybe it was the special lighting of the case that made his face look shadowed, as if it were hollowed with hunger . . . or avarice.

Then again, maybe the lighting had nothing to do with it.

Morgan paused in the doorway of the room and watched him silently, uneasy. The last few visitors in this area wandered past her, talking, and she nodded automatically at one of the guards who was following his usual patrol past the room, but she could hardly take her eyes off Quinn.

Max Bannister, certainly nobody's fool and a notable judge of character, believed this man saw his unique collection only as bait set out to lure a far more deadly thief. Wolfe was risking his job and sterling reputation because he believed the same thing—or because he trusted Max's judgment. Even Jared, despite the bitter anger he'd shown about his brother's life of crime, seemed to have no doubt that Quinn had no designs on the Bannister collection.

And Morgan had believed that as well. From the moment she'd been told he was working with Interpol in the attempt to capture another and more deadly thief, she hadn't doubted what he was here to do—even if she had wondered about his motives.

But now, watching him as he stared at the Bolling

diamond, she felt her throat close up and her hands were suddenly cold. His face was so still, his eyes oddly intent, and she couldn't help wondering . . .

Was the enigmatic Quinn making fools of them all?

Drawing a deep breath and then holding her clipboard rather like a shield, she moved slowly toward him. It was obvious he knew he'd been under observation because he spoke rather absentmindedly as soon as she reached him.

"Hello, Morgana. Do you know the history?"

"Of the Bolling?" She was pleased by her own calm voice. "No, not really, other than that it's supposed to be cursed. As director of the exhibit, my responsibilities are all administrative. I know, of course, all the facts about the pieces—carat weight and the grades of each stone, for instance—but I don't believe in curses, and gems were never my favorite subject."

"So, as an archaeologist you prefer relics? Bits of pottery and fossils?"

"Something like that."

He turned his head suddenly and smiled at her. "I thought diamonds were a girl's best friend."

"Not this girl. To be honest, I don't even like diamonds. Rubies, yes; sapphires and emeralds, definitely—but not diamonds, even the colored ones."

"Too hard? Too cold?" He seemed honestly curious.

"I don't know why, I've never thought about it." She shrugged off the subject. "How long have you been here?"

"Just a few minutes." He looked around them, his

expression critically assessing. "The design of the exhibit is excellent. My compliments."

"Being a connoisseur of such things?"

"I have closely studied a number of gem exhibits over the years," he reminded her modestly.

He had skillfully plundered a few as well. Morgan sighed. "Yeah. Well, I can't take all the credit for this one. Max and I designed the layout, but Wolfe and Storm had input because of security considerations and Dani helped with the lighting and display angles." She paused, then added, "I know you've met Storm because she said Wolfe introduced you last night; has Jared introduced you to Dani?"

Before he could answer, a serene and polite recording announced over the public address system that the museum would be closing in fifteen minutes. Quinn waited for the end of the announcement before nodding in reply.

"Yes, he has. Just before they got married last Sunday, as a matter of fact. I trust they'll have better luck this time around."

"Then you didn't know her when they were married before."

Quinn turned fully to face her. He was smiling slightly, but in the low light of the exhibit his green eyes seemed shuttered. "No. Ten years ago I was finishing up college—here in the States."

"I wondered why you didn't have much of an accent," Morgan commented. And then, since he seemed willing to provide some information about his past, she said, "I guess you've kept your distance from Jared since then. With him being a cop, I mean."

Instead of responding to that, Quinn said, "We are dissimilar brothers, aren't we? Jared said he let that slip the night I was shot. He also said he asked you to forget you'd heard it."

"It was more of a command than a request," Morgan said, not sure if she had touched a nerve or if Quinn was merely being evasive for some other reason. Or even if he was being evasive at all. "I don't respond too well to commands."

"Noted for future reference," Quinn murmured.

She had to resist the urge to follow *that* interesting tangent, and though it was hard, she managed. "Isn't it dangerous, given the circumstances, to have so much tension between you two?"

"Not at all. We're both pros." In a smooth motion, Quinn took her arm, turned her, and headed toward the doorway. "The museum's closing, didn't you hear? It might look a bit strange if you don't leave as usual."

Morgan knew a warning sign when one was raised in front of her, so she dropped the subject of his relationship with his brother. For the time being, at least. "Do you think he's watching the museum? Nightshade, I mean?"

"I have no idea," Quinn confessed cheerfully. "But if I were him, I'd already have my plans made. And since we know he's spent at least one night casing the building, it's a safe bet that he has. The trick is going to be trying to anticipate what he means to do—and when."

"I don't see how you can do that. How anyone could."

Still lightly holding her elbow as he guided her out of the west wing and toward the central staircase, Quinn shrugged. "Since I'm not psychic, it's going to have to be an educated guess based on what I know about Nightshade's methods and past thefts. Which is to say . . . very little."

"You're instilling me with a lot of confidence."

He chuckled at her sarcasm. "Don't worry, Morgana—one way or another, I always land on my feet."

And with the gems? But she didn't say that aloud. Instead, she said, "Are you going to keep watch tonight?"

"From midnight on. Jared will watch until then; we've split the duty between us."

Morgan glanced up at him as they went down the stairs to the lobby. "I guess you're used to staying up all night, huh?"

Quinn uttered another low laugh. "Let's just say that I seem to be living the life of a vampire—never in bed before dawn and seldom up before sunset."

His analogy was a bit too close to her earlier musings for Morgan's peace of mind, and she had to stop herself from reaching for the cross at her throat. For heaven's sake! Just because the man was charming and enigmatic—and worked nights—didn't make him Dracula!

"The sun's still out, you know," she heard herself

saying, and was relieved that her voice was dry. "Aren't you afraid you'll burst into flame or turn into dust?"

"No, but these long summer days must be hell on real vampires," he noted thoughtfully.

"Real—" Morgan got hold of herself. "I've been watching creepy movies on cable lately; what's your excuse?"

"Too many nights spent clinging to the side of a building like a bat," he replied matter-of-factly, then went on with scarcely a pause. "Morgana, I'm in the mood for Italian food, I think, and I know of a great restaurant near the bay with the best cook this side of Naples. Will you join me?"

He had stopped in the lobby about halfway between the guards' desk and the main doors, and even when he released her elbow, Morgan had the curious feeling that he was still touching her. With an effort, she shook off the sensation.

Bluntly, she asked, "Business or pleasure?"

He answered that readily and with a smile. "Your company is always a pleasure, sweet. However, I'll admit there is a possibility that someone I'd like to keep an eye on will also be at the restaurant."

"Who?"

"That, I'd rather not say." When she frowned at him, Quinn added, "Suspicions are not facts, Morgana, and they're a long way from evidence. I'd prefer not to name names—to anyone—until I'm sure."

"You mean not even Max or Jared—or Wolfe—knows that you have an idea who Nightshade really is?"

"They know I have an idea," Quinn conceded, "but they don't know who I'm watching."

There were a number of questions Morgan wanted to ask, but a glance around showed her that they were alone in the lobby except for a guard at the desk who was watching them unobtrusively, so she decided this was not the time or place for a long discussion.

"Italian food sounds great," she said. "I'll just go check on a couple of things and get my jacket."

"I'll wait here for you."

Since she was a responsible and efficient woman, Morgan made two brief stops before reaching her office, checking with the guards in the security room and then with Storm in the computer room to make certain all was well as the museum went into a night-security mode. One of the guards watching the security monitors asked her if the blond man in the lobby was supposed to be on his "sheet"—meaning the list of persons with special clearance to enter the museum at will—and Morgan had to pause for thought before answering.

"No," she said finally out of a sense of caution, but then qualified the reply by adding, "Not unless Max or Wolfe says so. But he'll probably be around most days. His name is Alex Brandon, and he's a collector. Ask Wolfe what his clearance is, will you?"

"Gotcha," the guard replied, writing himself a note.

When Morgan stopped at the computer room, where Storm spent her working hours, it was to find the petite blonde leaning back in her chair, booted feet propped on her desk and her little cat asleep in her lap as she studied a video monitor hanging in the corner of the crowded room. She could use the computer console on her desk to direct the museum's security program to show her any part of the museum under video surveillance, and at that moment she was looking at the lobby. Specifically, at a tall, blond man waiting patiently.

"Hi," Morgan said, deciding not to comment. "Any problems before I go?"

"Nah, nothing to speak of. I've fixed that glitch in the system, so I doubt we'll have any more accidental alarms." Storm's bright green eyes returned to their study of the monitor, and she smiled when Quinn turned his own gaze to look directly into the video pickup he wasn't supposed to be able to see. "Look at that. When he got here a little while ago, I watched him all through the museum, and he always knew where the cameras were—even the ones we've so cleverly hidden. Wolfe says he has a sixth sense when it comes to any kind of a camera being pointed at him, that he feels it somehow. No wonder the police have never been able to capture him on tape or film."

Morgan followed her friend's gaze, and though she couldn't help a rueful smile when Quinn winked cheerily at the camera, her voice held a certain amount of frustration. "Damn him. Just when I think I've got him figured out, I start having second thoughts. Is he on the right side of the law this time, or isn't he?"

Storm looked at her, one brow on the rise. "Maybe

the operative phrase in that question is 'this time.' Even if you give him the benefit of the doubt and assume Max, Wolfe, and Jared are right to trust him to keep his hands off the collection—and none of them are fools, we both know that—then what's he going to do afterward? Let's say our little trap works and Nightshade winds up behind bars—what then? Does Quinn slip Interpol's leash and fade back into the misty night? Does he go to prison for past crimes? Or is the plan for him to be a . . . consultant or something like that for the cops?"

Remembering an earlier discussion with Quinn, Morgan said, "He told me he was too effective to go public—which would mean a trial and possibly prison—and more or less said he enjoyed dancing to Interpol's tune. Which is probably the only answer I'll get."

Storm pursed her lips thoughtfully and stroked the sleeping Bear with a light touch. "Shrewd of Interpol if they plan to make good use of his talents."

"Yeah. He's sure to be worth more to them outside a jail than in. Even if they never recover a thing he stole, I'll bet they'd rather use him than prosecute." Morgan sighed. "Which only tells me one thing. Interpol operates mostly in Paris and other parts of Europe—and so would he."

"How's your French?" Storm asked solemnly.

"Better than my Latin."

"I could give you lessons," the blonde offered.

Morgan eyed her. "Do you speak French with a southern accent?"

"According to Jared I do, but I've never had any trouble being understood."

"Well, I may take you up on the offer," Morgan said. "Then again, the only French word I'm likely to need to know is the one for good-bye. And I already know that one." She shook her head before her friend could respond. "Never mind. I'm going to eat Italian food and try my best to remember all the logical, rational, sensible reasons why I shouldn't lose my head."

"Good luck," Storm murmured.

Morgan went on to her office, where she deposited her clipboard on her desk and put on the stylish gold blazer she had worn that morning. Then she locked up her office and returned to where Quinn waited in the lobby.

Wolfe was there and talking to him as she approached; she couldn't hear what the security expert was saying, but he was frowning a bit. Quinn was wearing a pleasant but noncommittal half smile; that seemed his only response to whatever he was being told. When he caught sight of Morgan, Quinn looked past Wolfe to watch her coming toward them, and Wolfe turned to address her rather abruptly.

"Will you be here tomorrow?"

"With the exhibit open? Sure. From now until we close up shop, I work six days a week."

Wolfe lifted an eyebrow at her. "Does Max know about that?"

"We've discussed the matter." Morgan smiled. "He wasn't happy, but when I pointed out that I'd be here whether I was getting paid or not, he gave in. I'm under orders to take long lunches and knock off early whenever possible, and I'm forbidden to darken the doors on Sunday. Why, do you need me for something tomorrow?"

"I'll let you know."

"Okay," she murmured, wondering if Wolfe felt uncomfortable discussing security business with her in the presence of Quinn. If so, it was certainly understandable.

Wolfe glanced at Quinn, then at Morgan, seemed about to say something, but finally shook his head in the gesture of a man who was acknowledging that a situation was out of his hands. "Have a nice evening," he said a bit dryly, and left them to head for the hall of offices.

Gazing after the darker man, Quinn said meditatively, "Do you get the feeling Wolfe isn't entirely happy with any of us?"

"Yes, and I can't blame him. Anything happens to the Bannister collection and Lloyd's is on the hook for more millions than I even want to think about."

Quinn took her arm and began guiding her toward the front doors. "True. Have I mentioned, by the way, that you look like a few million yourself today?"

It caught her off guard—*damn* the man for sounding unnervingly sincere without warning!—but Morgan recovered quickly and was able to reply with commendable calm as they walked across the pavement outside the museum. "No, you haven't mentioned that." There was a little sunlight left in the day, and it glinted off his pale gold hair very nicely, she decided absently.

"Well, you certainly do. You look ravishing in jeans, mind you, but this is very elegant." He guided her toward the low-slung black sports car waiting at the curb.

"Thank you." Wondering if he did this kind of thing deliberately just to keep her off balance, Morgan remained silent while he installed her in the passenger side. She waited for him to join her, and spoke only when the little car pulled away from the curb with a muted roar.

"Answer a question for me?"

He sent her a quick smile. "I'll have to hear it first."

"Umm. Do you know the security layout of the museum—and the exhibit?" She had wondered about that only after Storm had made the observation that he "sensed"—or knew—the placement of all the security video cameras.

"Do you really think Jared would be so trusting?"

"That," she commented thoughtfully, "is not an answer."

Quinn chuckled softly. "Morgana, I get the distinct feeling I've somehow roused your suspicions."

"That isn't an answer either. Look, Alex, we've agreed that the truth seems to be a slippery commodity between the two of us." She half turned on the seat to study his profile. It was a good profile, which was inspiring—but not as regards clarity of thought. "So

I'd appreciate it if you give me a direct answer whenever possible. If you'd rather not say, then tell me so—this habit you have of neatly evading various subjects is not calculated to persuade me to trust you."

"Yeah, I was afraid of that." Stopping the car at a traffic light, he glanced at her a bit more seriously. "I'll try not to do that so often."

She noticed he didn't promise to stop doing it. "So . . . do you or don't you know the security setup of the exhibit?"

"I don't. I probably could have gotten it from Max—who does trust me, by the way—but I decided not to. I have a better chance of anticipating Nightshade if I have to study the museum and exhibit just the way he does. The only advantage I have is that I *know* there's a weakness in the defenses."

"The trap? Is it Storm's security program?"

"You don't know?"

Morgan sighed. "I'm ashamed to admit it, but I haven't even asked."

In an understanding tone, Quinn said, "The situation *is* a bit complicated."

"Never mind. Do you know where the trap is?"

"Yes, I do. I told Wolfe in the lobby just before you joined us, and he confirmed my deductions."

"No wonder he was frowning."

"As I said, he isn't very happy with any of us. I did point out to him that the trap only *looks* like a hole in the defenses, expressly designed to lure Nightshade in and snare him before he can get anywhere near the collection."

"And was he mollified by this reminder?"

Quinn smiled. "No. He seemed to feel that Nightshade might be suspicious enough to avoid the trap and find his own way in."

"Why would he be suspicious?"

"Because of me, I'm afraid." He sighed. "Morgana, thieves don't normally follow one another in the dead of night. But I followed him the night he was casing the museum, the night he shot me. He has to wonder about that. He knows he didn't kill me, because no unexplained shootings have been reported in the city, so he knows I may still be a potential problem."

"But he doesn't know who you are," Morgan said slowly.

"I'm an unanswered question all the way around—and a man like Nightshade hates unanswered questions."

She frowned a little as she studied his face. "You know, every time you talk about Nightshade, I get the feeling there's more to this. You say you don't know much about him . . . but I think you do."

"Morgana, you are full of questions today."

"Is that a warning?"

"It's an observation."

It may have been only that, but Morgan decided to drop the subject anyway. Quinn had already been more forthcoming than she had expected, and she preferred to quit while she was ahead. In any case, they arrived at the restaurant just then, and a number of speculations filled her mind.

She didn't comment until he had parked the car and come around to open her door, and when she did speak, it was in a dry tone. "So Tony's is the best restaurant this side of Naples, huh?"

"I think so," Quinn replied innocently as he closed her car door and took her arm.

"And I suppose the fact that it tends to be a kind of hangout for art collectors and dealers as well as museum people is a coincidence?"

He sent her a glance, amusement in his green eyes. "No, is it? Fancy that."

"You can be maddening, you know that?"

"Watch your step, Morgana," he murmured, probably referring to the uneven flagstone steps leading up to the restaurant's front door.

Though it was not yet seven in the evening, the place was already three quarters full; many of the museums in the area closed at six, and this was, as Morgan had said, a favorite place to unwind as well as dine. The food was not only excellent, it was also served generously and priced reasonably, and the casual but efficient waitresses knew your name by the third visit.

Or, in Quinn's case, the second.

"I ate lunch here Wednesday," he told Morgan, after the friendly waitress had conducted them to a window booth and asked "Mr. Brandon" if he wanted coffee as usual.

Morgan—who was also known to the waitress and who had ordered coffee as well—accepted that somewhat ruefully with a nod and then glanced around casually, curious to see if she could spot whoever it was that Quinn wanted to keep an eye on.

The one glance told her it would be impossible. There were more than a dozen people scattered about the room who were in some way involved in the art world either as collectors, patrons, or employees of the various museums, galleries, and shops in the area. Even Leo Cassady, their host for the party the previous night, and Ken Dugan, curator of the museum housing the Mysteries Past exhibit, were present, both with attractive female companions. And she was almost sure she'd spotted Keane Tyler, an inspector with the San Francisco police, eating alone in a dim corner.

"Give up?" Quinn murmured.

Morgan unfolded her napkin and placed it over her lap, making a production out of it. "I don't know what you're talking about," she told him politely.

"You mean you weren't trying to guess who it is I'm keeping an eye on?" He smiled wickedly. "Nice try, sweet, but you should never try to play poker with a cardsharp."

She scowled at him. "Thanks for yet another warning. Obviously, you could look as innocent as a lamb with both sleeves full of aces."

Leaning back to allow the waitress to place his coffee before him, Quinn said, "I didn't know lambs had sleeves."

"You know what I mean. *Your* sleeves full of aces."
Morgan reached for the sugar and poured a liberal
amount into her coffee, then added a generous measure
of cream.

Quinn watched her with a slightly pained expression on his handsome face. "American coffee is filled
with flavor; why do you want to turn it into dessert?"

Since he'd stayed at her apartment, Morgan knew
how he took his coffee. "Look, just because you macho
types think drinking something incredibly bitter is a
gourmet experience doesn't make it so."

"Is the coffee bitter?" the waitress asked anxiously.
"I'm so sorry."

Morgan looked up at her rather blankly, then realized the attractive redhead was hovering, pad in hand
and pencil poised, to take their orders for the meal.

"I can make a fresh pot—"

"No, it's fine." Morgan glanced at Quinn, who was
studying the menu with one of those maddening little
smiles of his, then returned her gaze to the distressed
waitress. "Really it is. I was just . . . trying to make a
point." She hastily picked up her menu.

A couple of minutes later, their meal ordered and
the waitress departed for the kitchen, Morgan frowned
at her companion. "It didn't work."

"What didn't work?"

"Trying to lead me off on a tangent. Maybe I
should start guessing who it is you're watching."

"So I can tell you if you're hot or cold?" Quinn
shook his head. "Sorry, Morgana—no deal."

She felt frustrated, but not terribly surprised, and since he *was* a much better poker player than she was, she knew there was no use in hoping he'd tell her anything he didn't want her to know. "Well, hell," she said in disgust.

Quinn smiled, but his eyes were suddenly grave. "Suppose you found out that I believed someone you knew was an international thief and murderer. Could you look at them, speak to them, with the ease you had yesterday? Could you be sure that you wouldn't inadvertently give away your knowledge or somehow put them on their guard—which would certainly ruin our plans and likely put you in danger? Could you, Morgana?"

After a moment she sighed. "No, I don't think I could. I'm not that good an actress."

"If it makes you feel any better, that's the major reason I haven't told any of the others. Because it takes a certain kind of nerve—or a devious nature, I suppose—to lie convincingly even under the stress of facing a killer. I know myself; I know that I *can* do that. And since I can't be so sure of anyone else, I prefer not to take the risk."

"But it is someone I know? Nightshade is?"

"Someone you know . . . if I'm right."

Morgan gazed at him soberly. "I get the feeling that no matter what you say—you don't have any doubts."

Quinn's humorous mouth quirked in an oddly self-mocking little smile. "Which ought to teach me a lesson. I'm obviously not the poker player I thought I was."

"Your face didn't give it away. Or even what you

said," Morgan answered absently. "Just something I felt. But you are sure, aren't you? You know who Nightshade is?"

"I can't answer that."

"You mean you won't."

"All right, I won't." Quinn sighed. "Morgana, in the interest of our developing relationship, why don't we make an agreement?"

"Such as?"

"Let's say . . . anytime we're together, we can discuss business only during the first hour. After that, we concentrate on us. Fair enough?"

"On us? You mean, regular old boy-meets-girl sort of stuff?" When he nodded, Morgan eyed him thoughtfully—but this time she wasn't picking up anything that belied his words. She had to accept them at face value, at least for the time being.

"Well?"

"It sounds fair enough. Always supposing, of course, that nothing exciting is going on around us. Museums being burgled or the two of us getting ourselves locked in an abandoned building, or getting shot at, for instance."

Gravely, he agreed, "Excepting those circumstances, of course."

"In that case, I agree." She sighed. "I think I've been manipulated by a masterly hand, but I agree."

Quinn didn't comment on her reservations; he merely nodded, still grave. "Good. Then we have the evening before us. Until midnight."

"I thought I was supposed to say that."

He grinned at her. "In this version of the story, the horses don't turn into mice, the carriage into a pumpkin, or your dress into rags."

"You just turn into Quinn." She kept her voice low when she said that, even though there was no one near them.

"I could be much worse, you know," he said in a soothing tone. "I could be dull." He reached across the table and touched the back of her hand very lightly, his index finger tracing an intricate pattern.

For a moment Morgan watched what he was doing, using every ounce of her self-control to preserve a detached expression, even though she had the suspicion all her bones were melting. She had to slide her hand away from him before she dared to meet his eyes, and she was rather proud when her voice emerged dryly.

"Alex, do you know the definition of a scoundrel?"

His green eyes were brightly amused. "A villain with a smile?"

"Close enough," Morgan replied with a sigh, and leaned back to allow the waitress to deliver their meal.

FOUR

It was nearly two in the morning when Quinn moved ghostlike along the dark, silent building until he reached a side door. There was no lock to bar his way, and within seconds he was passing along a dim hallway, still making no more noise than a shadow. He paused outside a heavily carved set of doors and studied the faint strip of light visible at the floor, then smiled to himself and entered the room.

The faint light came from only two sources: a cheerful fire burning in the rock fireplace and a reading lamp on the opposite side of the study. Still, it was easy for Quinn to see the room's waiting occupant.

"You're late." His host turned away from a tall window to frown at him.

Quinn removed his black ski mask and the supple black gloves he wore, and tucked them into his belt. "There's quite a bit of security in this neighborhood, so I had to be careful," he responded calmly.

The other man didn't cross the room or even move away from the window; he merely stood there, one hand on the back of the chair beside him, and looked at Quinn. "Did you get it?"

Silently, Quinn opened a chamois pouch at his belt and removed a smaller velvet bag, which he tossed to his host. "As you Yanks say—it was a piece of cake." Subtly different from what Morgan was accustomed to hearing from him, his voice was more rapid than lazy, the words a bit more clipped, the pronunciation more British than American.

A brilliant cascade of diamonds flowed into the other man's hand as he upended the velvet bag, and he stared down at the necklace without blinking for a long moment. Then, softly, he said, "The Carstairs diamonds."

"Get out your loupe and satisfy yourself the necklace is genuine," Quinn advised him. "I don't want there to be any question."

His host left the window finally to cross the room to an antique desk, and he removed a jeweler's loupe from the center drawer. He turned on the desk lamp to provide more light, and under that studied the necklace thoroughly.

"Well?" Quinn asked when the other man straightened.

"It's genuine."

"Terrific." Quinn's deep voice held a faint trace of mockery, as if the other man's terseness amused him.

"So, are we ready to talk about the Bannister collection now?"

"I told you, I don't like the setup."

"Neither do I." Quinn sat casually on the arm of a leather wingback chair and gave his host a very direct look. "The exhibit has the best security money can buy—which shouldn't surprise either one of us. But we both know that even the best security is little more than an illusion to help owners and insurance companies sleep at night. No system is foolproof."

The other man's eyes were suddenly hard and bright. "Have you found a way in?"

Quinn smiled. "I've found two ways in."

". . . and then he took me home," Morgan told Storm, finishing a rather lengthy description of her date the previous night. "And he didn't even ask to come in for coffee."

"That cad," Storm said solemnly.

Morgan stared at her friend for a moment, then giggled. "Did I sound aggrieved?"

"Just a little bit."

"Well, I guess I am a little bit." Sitting on the edge of Storm's desk, Morgan frowned as she absently scratched Bear under his raised chin. "After I'd finally come to the conclusion that I really would be stupid to trust him, he was as perfect gentleman all evening. At dinner, at the concert, in the car. He was charming, he was a wonderful companion, and he never put a foot wrong."

In her usual pose, leaning back in her chair with her booted feet propped up on the desk, Storm watched the dark woman with a little smile. "Did he ask you out again?"

Morgan nodded. "For tonight, as a matter of fact. When I told him I'd decided weeks ago not to go to that fund-raiser Ken's organized, he asked if I'd change my mind and go with him. I heard myself saying yes before I had a chance to think it through." She shook her head. "You know, for someone who's officially been in San Francisco only since Wednesday, he sure has all the hot tickets."

"A man who plans ahead, obviously."

"Yeah—and it makes me very nervous." Morgan sighed and got off the desk. She went to the door, but paused there to look at her friend somewhat bemusedly. "You know what he wants to do tomorrow? He wants to go to the zoo. And have a picnic."

"That sounds like a nice way to spend a Sunday," Storm observed in a grave voice.

"It sounds like a *normal* way to spend a Sunday. Am I the only one who finds that somewhat bizarre?"

"It's not at all bizarre for someone like Alex Brandon. But that other guy you met in a dark museum one night might find a normal Sunday a bit . . . quaint."

Morgan nodded, slowly, seriously. "It is like he's two different men."

"And you feel ambivalent about one of them?"

"Oh, no, that isn't the problem." Morgan's voice was certain. "I find both of them too fascinating for my peace of mind. What really bothers me is that the one I trust . . . is the man who wears a ski mask."

"That," Storm said, "is very interesting."

"It's unnerving, that's what it is." Sighing, Morgan added, "I've got to go and check on the exhibit. See you later."

A man in the crowd of museum visitors whistled under his breath when Morgan passed him on her way up to the exhibit, and she threw him a faintly surprised glance. She was dressed more casually than yesterday, though still elegantly, in silky black pants and a bulky cowl-neck sweater in a bright shade of gold, with her long hair in a French braid. To her mind, it was a comfortable and presentable outfit without being especially sexy, and the attention from a stranger startled her.

She returned the man's admiring smile with no more than polite acknowledgment and kept going— though he approached her five minutes later and made rather insistent let's-get-to-know-each-other-better noises. Experienced in that kind of situation, she managed to get rid of him without raising her voice or having to summon one of the guards—though the stranger retreated with a somewhat dazed look on his face.

It was an odd thing, but Morgan had found that strangers were more likely to ask her out than men who knew her. That had been a disconcerting realization, and one she hadn't quite been able to explain completely to her own satisfaction. She honestly didn't believe that men were turned off by her personality; she thought it was more a matter of their being initially misled by her appearance.

When a woman looked like a busty sex kitten, she'd long ago discovered, men seldom expected a forthright and often sardonic nature and *never* expected intelligence. So while an embarrassing number of strangers approached her in public with hopeful expressions, it seemed to require time for those who knew her to reconcile a centerfold appearance with a sharp mind and well-defined personality.

At least, that was the explanation Morgan had finally arrived at, and one that seemed to make sense. And believing that was certainly better than believing she had only to open her mouth to scare most men off. . . .

The remainder of Saturday morning was fairly calm, with no unexpected crises and only one minor problem—which was easily solved by another slight adjustment of the flow of traffic through the exhibit. After that, Morgan had little to do except be on hand and answer the occasional question from a visitor.

She returned to her office and left her clipboard there just before noon, planning to take a long lunch as she'd promised Max she would. She stopped at the door of the computer room when she went back down the hall, finding Wolfe there talking to Storm.

"Hi." Morgan frowned slightly at Wolfe. "Did you

want to talk to me about something? Yesterday in the lobby, I thought maybe you did."

Wolfe shook his head. "No, I was just going to suggest that we post a few more signs about not touching the glass of the display cases, but when you redirected the traffic flow this morning, that seemed to put a little extra space between the people and the cases."

Morgan nodded, but her gaze went from his face to Storm's and then back again. "Okay—so what else is wrong? You two look a bit grim."

"I never look grim," Storm objected. "Just . . . concerned."

"Why?" Morgan repeated.

It was Wolfe who answered. "Keane Tyler just called. The Carstairs diamonds were stolen last night."

Morgan leaned against the doorjamb and crossed her arms beneath her breasts. She was still frowning at Wolfe. "That's a shame, but why did he call you?"

"He thought we should know, and the theft won't be made public because that's the way the Carstairs want it. The necklace was in a safe at the Carstairs residence, but the security system was top of the line, maybe better than what we have here around the exhibit—and the thief waltzed through without tripping a single alarm. There were even guard dogs patrolling outside, and they never let out a whimper."

"Sound familiar?" Storm murmured.

"You don't think it was Quinn?" Morgan said.

"No," Wolfe responded immediately. But he

wasn't looking at her when he said it, and he was frowning.

In a dispassionate tone, Storm said, "We all know there are plenty of thieves in San Francisco. Especially right now. Just because this particular thief beat a dandy security system doesn't mean it was Quinn."

"Of course not," Morgan said, but she heard a hollow note in her own voice.

Wolfe did look at her then, still frowning. "Let's not jump to conclusions, any of us. That necklace has been a prime target for years, and the security system is months old—long enough for someone to have gotten their hands on the diagrams and found a weak spot."

"That's true," Storm agreed.

Morgan looked at them both, then said, "Yeah. Okay, well, let me know if Keane finds out anything. I'll be back in a couple of hours."

Wolfe started to say something, but Storm caught his eye and shook her head warningly. When they were alone a minute later, he said, "I was going to ask her to join us for lunch."

"I know." Storm smiled at him. "Excellent intentions, but bad timing." She nodded toward the monitor in the room, and when Wolfe turned to stare at it, he saw what she meant.

Quinn was standing in the lobby.

Morgan was so surprised when she saw him there that for a moment she forgot the disturbing news she'd just learned. "What're you doing here? It's barely noon."

Eerily burglarlike in a dark sweater and black slacks, he smiled and shrugged. "I couldn't sleep, so I decided to come and find out if I could take you to lunch."

Just once, I want to be able to say no to him. Just once.

"Sure," she said.

A couple of minutes later Morgan found herself in his little sports car, and by then she'd remembered Wolfe's troubling news. She didn't want to admit to the twinge of doubt she'd felt, but she couldn't help turning in the seat to study Quinn's face as she spoke in a deliberately casual tone.

"Ever heard of the Carstairs necklace?"

Somewhat dryly, he replied, "The same way I've heard of the Hope diamond. Who hasn't? Why?"

"It was stolen last night."

He let out a low whistle, and the only emotion his face showed was mild interest. "I'd like to know who managed that."

"It . . . wasn't you," she said, trying not to make it a question even though it was.

Quinn turned his head to look at her briefly, then returned his gaze to the road. "No. It wasn't me."

Morgan had the upsetting idea that she had hurt him. "I had to ask."

"I know."

"I'm sorry."

He glanced at her again, this time with a crooked

smile. "Why? We both know what I am. You'd have to be an idiot not to suspect me, Morgana—and you aren't an idiot. Besides that, trust is something we're working *toward*—remember?"

"I just wish . . ."

"What?"

"Well, I just wish Nightshade would make his move and get it over with. I don't think I can stand waiting for the next two months."

"Somehow, I doubt he'll wait so long. The Bannister collection will be impossible for him to resist, believe me. I'd be very surprised if he waits as much as two weeks before making an attempt."

"Intuition? Or experience?"

"A bit of both, I suppose." Quinn sent her another quick smile. "That's why I'm here, remember? To provide an expert's point of view. Set a thief to catch a thief?"

She sighed. "I wish you didn't sound so damned pleased about that."

"Never mind," he said with a chuckle. "You'll feel better after lunch."

Morgan nodded and then looked around to see where they were going. "Tony's?"

"I thought so, unless you have another preference."

"No, that's fine. Alex?"

"Hmm?"

"The night we met—you stole a dagger from that museum."

"Yes, I did," he agreed calmly.

"I don't suppose you returned it later?"

"No."

He sounded a little amused, Morgan thought, and wondered if she seemed to him incredibly naive. But she had to ask.

"And since then? If you *had* stolen anything else . . . would you tell me about it?"

Quinn turned the car into the parking lot at Tony's as he spoke, and his voice was very matter-of-fact. "No, Morgana, I wouldn't tell you." He pulled into a parking space, but paused before turning off the engine to look at her with a slight smile. "Still willing to have lunch with me?"

Looking into those vibrant green eyes, Morgan heard herself sigh and then heard herself say, "Sure."

She wasn't surprised. Neither was Quinn.

Damn him.

By the time they were together again that evening for the fund-raiser, Morgan had spent most of the day telling herself that getting involved with Quinn was not very smart. It was something else that didn't surprise her, because she'd been playing variations on that theme since the night she'd met him. And the self-advice didn't do any more good this time than it had during the past weeks.

It finally occurred to her, about the time she was getting dressed, that all the protests and doubts were intellectual—not emotional. *Emotionally* she'd made up her mind about Quinn a long time ago.

As long as she followed her instincts and emotions, she had no hesitation in trusting Quinn. She wasn't so sure about Alex Brandon, partly, she suspected, because she hadn't quite convinced herself he was a real person. A psychologist would no doubt have found that as interesting as Storm had, but the truth was that after hearing about him for years and having several rather dramatic nighttime encounters with him, "Quinn" was the most real man she had ever known.

In any case, since worrying about it wasn't doing her any good, Morgan decided to follow her instincts. This might well turn out to be an act of reckless folly, but if everybody deserved one of those, then maybe it was time for hers. Until she had literally run into Quinn in a dark museum more than two months ago, her life choices had been as practical as they'd been intelligent.

Not that she was complaining. Still, she felt more alive since she'd met him. And even if their relationship turned out to be as brief as the duration of Mysteries Past, it also promised to be as memorable as he was himself.

So why not enjoy herself?

In the past, Morgan had found that the fund-raisers she'd attended were either pleasant or incredibly boring; since the entire purpose was to raise money for some worthy cause (in this case to help out some of the private museums that had been burgled during the past weeks) a logical aim was to keep costs down. Ergo, the food tended to be banquet bland and the entertainment adequate rather than inspiring. So, to have a pleasant evening was to consider the event a success.

This particular fund-raiser had been organized by several museum curators—gentlemen not known for their adventurous spirits or love of the absurd—and their choice of entertainment was, to say the least, singular.

"It has a certain something," Quinn commented, leaning close to Morgan so she could hear him over the noise filling the large room. His expression was grave.

She winced at a discordant clash of notes from a band that seemed to have come from some twilight zone of amateur nights. "Oh, yeah, it has something. It has a beat and you can dance to it. But please don't ask me to."

He chuckled. "Well, we've done our duty. We listened to the speeches, ate the meal, and conversed intelligently with our table companions." He glanced around their table, which, like all the others in the room, seated twelve people—and was now deserted except for them and a very young couple on the other side who were totally wrapped up in each other.

"Most of whom bailed out half an hour ago," Morgan pointed out, half closing her eyes as the enthusiastic drummer showed off his talents.

Quinn leaned even closer to her and, his breath warm against her neck, said, "I think they all showed good sense. Why don't we follow suit? It's a beautiful night, and I happen to know of a coffee shop about two blocks from here. What do you say? We can walk off that mystery chicken dish and get some fresh air—and a decent cup of coffee."

Morgan was in complete agreement, though she did feel a bit guilty in joining the exodus from the building. "I should find Ken and tell him he did a good job," she said to Quinn.

"Tell him Monday at the museum," he suggested. "It'll give you time to construct a really sincere face."

She couldn't help laughing as they got up. "Is nothing sacred to you?"

Guiding her through the jungle of pushed-back chairs and the occasional—and inexplicable—dancers, Quinn said, "In the area of manners and mores, you mean? Sure. I just happen to believe we should all be completely honest with ourselves—especially when we have to lie to be polite to others."

Morgan thought about that while they made their way from the hotel that was hosting the fund-raiser. Since neither of them had worn coats—Quinn was in a black tux and Morgan's outfit consisted of black pants and a gold top worn with a fitted jacket—they didn't have to join the long line stretching out from the coat check, and in just a few minutes they'd reached the pavement outside the front of the hotel.

"Can you manage in those heels, or should I get the car?" Quinn asked.

"Which way are we going?"

The hotel was partway up one of the many hills in the city, but not a particularly steep one, and when Quinn pointed, it was downhill.

"I can manage a couple of blocks," she assured him, and took his arm when it was gravely offered.

As they strolled along the sidewalk Morgan agreed with him silently that it was a beautiful night. No rain, no fog, and no more than a slight breeze. It was cool without being chilly, and the city looked bright and colorful. A perfect night for a peaceful walk.

"You're very quiet, Morgana. Something wrong?"

She looked at her hand resting lightly on his arm, then drew in a breath of the clear night air and turned her gaze ahead of them again. "No, I was just thinking. Are you always honest with yourself, Alex?"

"Anyone who plays . . . identity games has to be."

"Identity games," she repeated slowly. "Is that what you do?"

He was silent for a moment, then spoke in an unusually serious tone. "I could say that when I was a boy I could never decide what I wanted to be when I grew up, but that wouldn't be true. What is true is that I had certain . . . talents that were not exactly suitable for your average career."

"Such as?" She thought he would say something about opening locks or blending into the night, but his answer was far more complex.

"The ability to reinvent myself whenever I had to. The ability to function well under . . . unusual kinds of pressure. The ability to work completely alone—and a liking for it." He shrugged. "I don't know what I might have done, but in college a friend dared me to . . . liberate something from the dean's house one night. I did it. And I liked it."

Morgan looked up at him curiously. "A college prank is a long way from professional burglary."

He smiled. "True."

"Was there any one thing that . . . bridged that distance? Something that happened to you, I mean."

"A tragedy that propelled me into a life of crime?"

She couldn't help but smile. "I said something like that once, didn't I?"

"Yes. And you were right to be doubtful of it." They had reached the coffee shop by then, and Quinn stopped on the sidewalk and turned to look down at her with a faint, rueful smile. "It was nothing so . . . romantic or quixotic, sweet, not a decision made in the heat of some painful or overwhelming emotion. I made a conscious, carefully thought out, cold-blooded choice. No apologies. No regrets."

Morgan sighed and let go of his arm. "I need a cup of coffee."

His smile went even more crooked. "I'm not making it easy for you, am I?"

"No. But then—you never said you would." She tried to sound humorous about it.

Quinn gazed at her upturned face for a moment, then bent his head and kissed her. It was a brief kiss but by no means light, and Morgan would have melted against him except that his hands were on her shoulders holding her still. When he lifted his head rather abruptly, she had the dazed impression that he said something a bit profane under his breath, but she didn't quite catch it.

He turned her briskly toward the door of the coffee shop and said, "You may not have realized, but it's nearly eleven."

Morgan allowed herself to be steered, but she heard the telltale frustration in her voice when she said, "Can't you take a night off?"

"Not this night—but I'll see what I can do about the future."

Once they were inside and seated at a small table in the crowded shop, Morgan wasn't quite sure which way the conversation would go, but Quinn was definite. To her surprise, he wanted to talk about her.

"My family?" She looked at him bemusedly. "Why do you ask?"

"It's all a part of the boy-meets-girl stuff," he told her in a grave tone. "I just realized I know practically nothing about your background."

So, still a little mystified, Morgan briefly described a life that, to her, had always seemed quite ordinary. A middle-class upbringing as an only child; her parents' deaths in a car accident when she was eighteen and the modest inheritance that had put her through college; summer archaeological digs in various parts of the world; the jobs and positions she'd taken over the years.

"You've been alone a long time," he noted.

She nodded. "I guess—six years since college." Gazing at him steadily, she added in a deliberate tone, "I was briefly engaged once, the summer before graduation."

"What happened?"

Morgan had never told anyone about this, but she found the words coming easily now, so easily that it startled her. "He was another archaeology student, we seemed to have everything in common. I thought so, anyway. But there were warning signs . . . and I should have paid attention."

"Warning signs?"

"Umm. He liked to see me dress a certain way—in clingy sweaters, for instance, and short skirts. His thoughts and opinions seemed to be more important than mine. In fact, he never wanted to talk to me about anything that mattered to me—even archaeology. He was always telling me I should wear my hair up, or use more eye makeup, or a different perfume."

Morgan shook her head and managed a smile. "Eventually I realized that who I was didn't matter to him—just what I looked like. And how I looked on his arm. He thought all his friends envied him because I looked . . ."

"Sexy?" Quinn supplied quietly.

"I guess. It was something I didn't want to believe about him, that he could be so . . . superficial. But when we went back to school in the fall for our senior year, they gave us an IQ test."

"And you scored higher than he did?" Quinn guessed.

Morgan looked down at her coffee cup, frowning a little as she remembered. "Twenty points higher. At first, he didn't believe it. He kept saying somebody must have screwed up the test. I finally lost my temper and told him I'd scored high before, and that the results were accurate. Then he—he just looked at me in shock. His eyes moved up and down over me in total incredulity, and he couldn't seem to say a word. So I did. I gave him back his ring and said good-bye."

"Morgana?"

She looked across the table at Quinn.

"Any man who could look at you and not see the intelligence and vitality in your eyes would have to be either blind or incredibly stupid." His own eyes laughed suddenly. "Of course, he'd also have to be blind or made of stone not to notice that you do look splendid in clingy sweaters."

Morgan couldn't help laughing, but she responded seriously to what she sensed was a serious point of his. "That experience made me wary—but not especially bitter. Noticing someone's looks is an automatic thing, after all, so I can hardly blame people for noticing mine. Obviously it's a problem only when they can't get past appearances." She paused, then added, "But you must admit that in me the . . . inner and outer woman are more than usually contradictory."

Quinn looked thoughtful. "As far as first impressions go, that may be true. But your mind, Morgana, is one of the most fascinating things about you. And the more I see of you, the more . . . complete the picture is."

"I *think* that was a compliment," she said cautiously.

He smiled. "It was."

"Then thank you." For the first time Morgan felt a bit self-conscious. "Shouldn't we be going? It must be after eleven, and if you have to—go to work—at midnight . . ."

A few minutes later, as they were walking back toward his car, Quinn said, "I'll pick you up around ten tomorrow morning, all right? The zoo first, then our picnic. My hotel provides catered lunches, so I'll see what they can do with a wicker basket."

"Ten? That won't leave you much time to sleep," she protested.

"I'll be fine, don't worry." He unlocked his car and opened the passenger door for Morgan, then went around and got in the driver's side. "I don't need much sleep."

Morgan thought about that later after he left her—with a kiss so light she wasn't sure she hadn't imagined it—at her door. She got out of her dressy clothes and into one of her sleep shirts, removed her makeup and took down her hair, then curled up on her couch with the television tuned to an old movie she stared at but didn't see.

Quinn would be on watch at the museum she thought. Dressed all in black, ski mask in place. Unarmed because he never carried a gun—at least according to what she'd read, and she made a mental note to ask him about that—and alone because that was the way he liked it. Throughout a long, chilly night.

How many nights before the trap succeeded—or

failed—to capture Nightshade? And what about afterward? She hadn't asked him that yet, and wasn't sure she would. Maybe it would be better just to wait and find out what the future would bring.

The problem was that patience wasn't one of Morgan's strongest traits. And nobody knew that better than she did.

Some distance away from Morgan's postmidnight contemplations and nowhere near the museum he was supposed to be watching, Quinn leaned forward in his comfortable chair and indicated a particular point on the diagrams spread out on the low coffee table.

"This is the glaring weakness, of course—this sealed, unused door near the basement storage rooms. But it's so far away from the exhibit, you'd be bound to trip a dozen alarms somewhere en route."

His host, who was standing beside his chair, nodded. "Yes, I know. You said there was another way?"

Quinn tapped the diagram again with a finger, this time indicating the building's air-conditioning system. "Here's a vulnerability. With the right preparation, you could make it work for you."

After a moment the other man nodded again. "Yes, I think I see what you're getting at."

"It's really very simple," Quinn said. "The system is almost foolproof. Almost. With so many security people—roaming guards and those in the lobby and security room—monitoring so much of the museum, it would be impossible to move more than a few feet down any corridor without being observed. But if you could immobilize all the guards *before* you entered the building, it would be a simple matter to get in through the basement and cut the building's main and backup power supplies—which would render all electronic security useless."

"There has to be an automatic alarm if the building loses power," the other man pointed out.

Quinn smiled. "There is. So you'd use a portable phone and call the monitoring security company—Ace Security—and report a glitch in the system. And since you'll know the private security code, they won't begin to worry until the system's been off-line for more than an hour. By then you'll be long gone."

"You have the code?"

"The code, the senior night guard's name *and* ID number—and an accurate diagram of the entire building's wiring."

The other man eyed him with a cold smile. "Congratulations. I would have sworn Morgan wouldn't let any of that slip even to a lover."

"I always have more than one source of information," Quinn explained calmly.

"But Morgan is one of them?"

Quinn leaned back in his chair and crossed one leg over the other casually. He was smiling. Coolly dispassionate, he said, "Morgan has been helpful to me in ways she couldn't even begin to imagine."

FIVE

By Monday, Morgan was half-convinced that Quinn's sole aim in life was to torment her. Never mind the Bannister collection or catching a thief; all he wanted to do was give her sleepless nights, chewed fingernails, and high blood pressure, to say nothing of gradual erosion of her sanity.

Sunday had been a case in point. First the zoo, where he had shown a love and appreciation of animals that had further weakened her defenses, and then the picnic. The picnic . . .

His hotel had provided a feast, he had brought along a thick blanket, and the weather cooperated by presenting them with a mild, dry day, generous sunlight, and a gentle breeze. The park they chose wasn't crowded even on such a nice day, so they had abundant privacy—considering they were out in the open—and since the other people who were there were simply strolling or having picnics of their own, it was quiet and peaceful.

As always, Morgan had felt completely comfortable with Quinn. Their conversation had been relaxed and casual, with him keeping the focus on her while they ate their lunch, asking more questions about her background and life. But after lunch, he was intent on a different kind of exploration.

Even on Monday morning, Morgan still felt weak in the knees and decidedly dazed when she remembered. He hadn't unfastened so much as a single button of her blouse, and his hands had never wandered anywhere that would have earned him a disapproving frown in church, yet he had managed to seduce her thoroughly with kisses. Never in her life had she felt anything like the melting, mindless desire he created in her. It had been emotional as well as physical, a craving so absolute she had felt possessed by it. And by him.

"You're doing this deliberately," she had accused him somewhat weakly when he had finally stopped kissing her. She was lying back on the blanket, which was a good thing; her legs would never have supported her.

Smiling as he stroked her hot cheek with steady fingers, but his eyes darkened and his voice more than a little raspy, Quinn had murmured, "Of course I'm doing it deliberately. I want you to want me, sweet."

She made a rather undignified sound of incredulous frustration when she heard his response, but she was beyond being embarrassed about it. She was just glad it had emerged wordlessly, because if she had said what she'd been thinking right then, she would still have been blushing on Monday.

I want you! When can I have you?

Although if she'd asked that blunt question, maybe he wouldn't have left her at her door late Sunday afternoon with no more than a brief kiss. Then again, maybe he would have.

"I have a lot to do this evening," he'd said apologetically before she could ask him to come in. "But I'll probably see you sometime tomorrow at the museum."

Not exactly a firm date, Morgan brooded on Monday. She thought about that—and him—all morning, driving herself crazy by recalling the day before. She delayed leaving for lunch just in case he showed up, and ended up eating alone at a café near the museum. (He was probably catching up on his sleep. Surely that was where he was.) When she went back to work, it was to find the museum crowded, a number of problems needing her attention—and no Quinn.

By four o'clock, when she was doing another walk-through of the exhibit, she was so preoccupied that she didn't even realize she was being paged over the public address system.

"Morgan?"

She tore her gaze from the display case holding the Bolling diamond and looked up to find Max standing beside her. "Oh. Hi, Max."

He was smiling faintly, but the perceptive gray eyes held concern. "Are you all right?"

She blinked. "Of course. Why?"

"We've been paging you for the last ten minutes."

Morgan conjured a smile. "Sorry. I guess my mind was . . . wandering. Is there a problem?"

"No. I've been talking to a reporter from the *Chronicle* about the exhibit, and she's brought a photographer to get some pictures—of us as well as the collection. So far the exhibit's been so successful that it seems we've become news."

Photographers . . . Her hair was loose today, which wasn't exactly businesslike or sophisticated, Morgan thought. She glanced down at what she was wearing, vaguely surprised to find herself in a short dark shirt and a long purple sweater. And purple high-heeled pumps. Purple? Odd. She couldn't remember owning any purple pumps. Where had she gotten them? Did she look presentable for a newspaper? She supposed so.

"Morgan?"

She looked up at Max again and was absolutely astonished to hear herself ask quite seriously, "Should I be wearing purple pumps?"

Max, a rare man who was not only never thrown by the unexpected but was also unusually discerning about people, replied without a blink. "I like them."

Morgan could feel her face getting hot. "Um. Good."

He smiled. "Is there anything you want to talk about?"

She lifted a hand to rub fretfully between her eyebrows, and discovered furrows there. Had she been frowning all day? "No, I don't think . . . no. Let's go get our pictures taken."

Max didn't pry. But Storm was a bit more curious when Morgan answered a question at random later that day and just before closing.

"I'll remember that if the need should arise," she told Morgan gravely in response.

"Remember what?" For the life of her, Morgan couldn't recall what she'd said. Or even what they'd been talking about.

"Where to buy a comfortable pair of purple pumps."

Morgan stared at her. "I don't suppose you asked me about shoes?"

"No. I asked if anyone had told you we'll be short one guard tonight."

Leaning somewhat weakly against the doorjamb of the computer room, Morgan mumbled, "God, I'm losing it."

"You do seem a bit distracted today," Storm agreed.

"Distracted? I'm *absent*. I have no idea what's happened around here today. Somebody could have walked off with the entire Bannister collection and I wouldn't have noticed a thing." She scowled. "Why will we be one guard short?"

"That stomach flu going around. Steve thought he could make it tonight, but his wife just called to say he's in bed and he's not going anywhere for a couple of days at least."

Morgan's frown deepened. "Any chance of getting a replacement from Ace?"

"Nope—they're coping with the flu too. Max said one guard more or less wouldn't matter, and Wolfe agreed. Neither of them wants to risk bringing in someone new to the museum, especially when we don't have time for thorough security clearances. I just wanted to make sure you knew about it."

"Thanks." Morgan glanced at her watch and sighed. "I think I'll take my purple pumps and go home."

"Maybe you'd better. Um . . . how was the picnic yesterday?"

Morgan could literally *feel* her eyes going unfocused and her face sort of wobble—and that was nothing compared with what happened to her knees. She closed her eyes and shook her head a little, trying to cast off the unnerving sensations.

"Wow," Storm murmured.

Opening her eyes cautiously, Morgan brought her friend into focus with tremendous effort. "It's just not right for a man to have this kind of effect on me. I don't suppose I could be coming down with the stomach flu?"

"I don't think so. What you've got won't run its course in forty-eight hours."

Morgan pushed herself away from the doorjamb, relieved to find her knees steady again, and conjured a smile. "No, but maybe I can learn to cope a bit better—at least to the point of not being so . . . out of control. A good night's sleep couldn't hurt. Like I said, I'm going to take my purple pumps and go home."

"See you tomorrow."

Morgan walked home, as usual. Four blocks. In heels. She stepped out of the shoes in the lobby of her apartment building and carried them up the stairs—the elevator was in the process of being repaired—to her third-floor apartment. Once inside, she threw the pumps in the general direction of her bedroom, turned her television on to hear the news, and went into the kitchen and put on a pot of coffee.

She didn't really think about what she was doing, just moved automatically. She fixed herself some supper, heating stew left over from the night before and cutting up a salad, and ate the meal without even tasting the food. Afterward, she cleaned the kitchen, then poured another cup of coffee and carried it into the living room.

It must have been around eleven-thirty that evening when Morgan's mind finally began working with something approaching her normal clarity, jarred by the fairly innocuous statement from Storm earlier.

You do seem a bit distracted today.

She sat there on her comfortable couch, still wearing the skirt and sweater but shoeless, her feet drawn up on the cushions, and scowled at the muted television. Slowly but inexorably, a fine, pure fury grew inside, filling her. It felt wonderful. Her mind was clear, her senses sharp, and for the first time in several days she knew she was looking directly at something he'd done his level best to distract her from seeing.

Damn him! That lousy, rotten, no-good thief had done it to her again. With all the skilled legerdemain of a master magician, he had convinced her that an illusion was real; she had been so intrigued—and seduced—by *Alex* that she had paid little attention to the nighttime activities of *Quinn*.

Oh, she'd asked the occasional mild question, but she hadn't really thought about the matter. And she should have. She really should have.

Characteristically, once anger took hold of her, Morgan didn't stop to think about what she was doing. She found a pair of black Reeboks and laced them swiftly onto her stockinged feet, caught up her purse, and left the apartment without even remembering to turn off the television.

Instead of rushing openly to the museum, she crossed the street and kept to the shadows, moving with all the stealth she could summon. She hung the strap of her shoulder bag across her chest so she was able to keep her hands free, but she was so intent on finding Quinn that she didn't follow her usual custom of keeping one cautious hand on her can of Mace.

It was easy enough to approach the museum without making her presence known, but once there, she had to figure out where Quinn would be keeping watch. None of her archaeological or administrative skills covered the problem of possible vantage points for cat burglars, so all she could depend on was her common sense.

He'd have to be high up, of course, with a clear view of the museum—but not so high that he couldn't get down in a hurry if he needed to, Morgan decided. She studied the buildings all around the museum, and finally settled on one that was only a couple of stories taller and less than half a block away. Once she got there, she found it was a perfect choice. An apartment building with a handy fire escape, it was in the process of being renovated and was obviously empty of tenants and curious doormen.

Five floors. Morgan gritted her teeth and climbed, trying to be quiet and silently cursing herself because she'd forgotten to bring a flashlight. The moon provided some light, but the angle of the fire escape kept her in total darkness most of the time. Which was, she decided later, the main reason he was able to catch her off guard.

It happened so quickly that Morgan had no time to yell. All of a sudden she was grabbed and yanked against a hard body, her arms pinned, and a cloth that smelled sickly-sweet covered her nose and mouth. She tried to struggle even as she fought to hold her breath, and she was vaguely aware that her heavy purse struck the metal of the fire escape with a sound that seemed incredibly loud.

By then her lungs were screaming for air, her nails clawing for any part of her attacker she could reach, and a sudden jolt of pain in one ankle told her she'd kicked the fire escape and had been punished for it. Dizziness swept over her, and as strength began to drain from her body she was conscious of a last, purely annoyed thought.

In all those old gothic romances, she remembered, the heroine always went charging off into the night, alone and unarmed, because she heard a suspicious sound or had a realization. Not only did she always land in trouble for it, but inevitably she was dressed in a filmy nightgown or something equally unsuitable for nighttime wandering.

Morgan had always sneered at those heroines, promising herself that *she* would never venture into danger with such a stupid lack of preparation. And, until now, she could say she'd been at least partially successful. After all, when she had gone charging (alone and unarmed) to Quinn's rescue sometime back when the bad guys had captured him, she had been sensibly dressed.

This time, she reflected irritably, she'd not only blundered out without the means to defend herself, but she hadn't even had the sense to put on a pair of jeans first.

She could feel her attacker's impressively hard body behind her, feel the ruthless strength of an arm that seemed to be cutting her in half, and she had the dim realization—a strange but comforting certainty—that it wasn't Quinn doing this to her. Then the chloroform did its work, and as she slumped against him she could feel her short skirt riding up her thighs.

Dammit, I should have put on some jeans. . . .

———◆————————◆———

She heard voices. Two of them, both male and both familiar to her. She was lying on something very hard and cold and uncomfortable, but she seemed to be wrapped in something like a blanket and she felt peculiarly safe. She couldn't open her eyes or even stir, but her hearing was excellent.

"Will she be all right?"

"Yeah, I think so. It was chloroform; the cloth was lying on the fire escape beside her."

"What the hell was she doing here?"

"Since she's been unconscious since I found her and before I called you, I've hardly been able to ask her."

"All right—then try this. What happened?"

"Look, I can only guess. Maybe he got suspicious of me and showed up tonight looking for me—either to watch me or to get rid of me. He had the chloroform with him, and I doubt he carries the stuff whenever he goes out; he was obviously planning to put somebody to sleep. Morgan must have surprised him coming up the fire escape. He couldn't get out of her way, so he had to get rid of her. If I hadn't heard something and gone down there to check it out, he might have had time to finish the job. She's damned lucky he didn't dump her over the railing and into the alley."

"All right, all right—calm down."

"I am perfectly calm," Quinn said in a voice so sharp it had edges.

Jared sort of sighed. "Yeah. Okay, we'll talk about this later. I gather I'm here to relieve you?"

"If you don't mind." Quinn gave a sigh as well—though his sounded a bit ragged. "I'm not expecting anything else to happen tonight, but I'm not sure enough to leave the place unwatched. I need to take Morgan back to her apartment and make sure she's going to be all right."

"No problem; I warned Dani not to expect me before morning."

"Thanks. Oh—you better keep the phone."

"Yeah." Abruptly, Jared sounded amused. "How're you going to get her home?"

"Carry her."

"Down five floors, across four blocks, and up another three floors?"

"She's not very big," Quinn replied a bit absently, his voice even clearer now because he had knelt beside her.

By that point, even if Morgan could have opened her eyes, she wouldn't have. Completely aware but utterly boneless, she felt herself gathered up and held in arms her body recognized instantly—simply by the touch of them. She heard an odd little noise escape her, something that sounded embarrassingly sensual, even primitive, and wondered uneasily if Jared heard her. Bad enough if Quinn heard . . .

She had the sensation of descending, though she heard nothing, and realized that Quinn managed to move almost silently even down a fire escape and carrying her. It made her feel very strange to be carried so effortlessly by him, and that probably delayed her recovery from the chloroform a good five minutes or more.

When Morgan finally managed to force her heavy eyelids up, the fire escape was behind them and Quinn was striding down the sidewalk right out in the open. She concentrated fiercely and managed to raise her head from his shoulder, and though the nausea was horrible, she managed not to get sick.

"I—I think I can walk," she told him, sounding decidedly weak to her own ears.

Quinn looked at her without breaking stride. His face was completely expressionless in the illumination of the streetlights, and his voice was unusually flat. "I doubt it. Your right ankle's badly bruised."

Since she was wrapped in a blanket, Morgan couldn't see her feet. She tried to move the right one experimentally and bit back a sound of pain. Remembering, she realized she must have banged that ankle hard against the fire escape in her struggles to escape her attacker.

Cradled in Quinn's arms, she gazed at his profile and wished miserably that she hadn't let her reckless anger make her go charging out after him. She'd had every right to be mad as hell, dammit, but now *this* had happened, and with him carrying her home—on her shield, so to speak—she felt ridiculously defensive and at fault. But then, even as the feelings surfaced, another realization made her feel a little better.

If she *hadn't* blundered into whoever that was on the fire escape, he might have been able to sneak up on Quinn—and he might not have simply put the cat burglar to sleep.

. . . *either to watch me or to get rid of me.*

Morgan shivered, and felt his arms tighten around her.

"Almost there," he said.

She let her head rest on his shoulder once more and closed her eyes against the waves of nausea. Apparently, feeling sick wasn't the only aftereffect of chloroform, because she dozed off again—only a few minutes this time. When she opened her eyes, Quinn was unlocking her apartment door. He must have at some point gotten her keys from her shoulder bag, she mused vaguely.

Inside the apartment, he lowered her to the couch so that she was sitting sideways, her feet up on the cushions. He was gentle enough, but she still caught her breath when her bruised ankle touched the firm cushions. The pain wasn't really horrible, but it turned sharp whenever she tried to move her foot or it touched anything.

Quinn straightened up and stared down at her, his face still curiously hard. In the subdued lighting of the living-room lamps, his green eyes were shuttered. He was dressed in his Quinn costume, black material from neck to toe, and as she looked up at him he dropped her keys onto the coffee table, then unbuckled his compact tool belt from around his waist and dropped it there as well.

He glanced at the television, which was still on and turned low, then looked at her again and said merely, "I'll get some ice for your ankle."

Alone in the quiet living room, Morgan managed to free her arms from the blanket. She found she was still carrying her shoulder bag and wrestled the strap off over her head; from the weight, she knew the only thing missing from it was her keys, so her attacker had obviously not attempted to rob her. She slung the bag onto the coffee table, and it landed on top of Quinn's tool belt.

A glance at the clock on her VCR told her it wasn't yet one A.M., which surprised her. How could so much happen in so little time?

Listening to the rattle of ice cubes in her kitchen, she cautiously leaned forward and opened the blanket the rest of the way to expose her legs, and winced at the sight of her right ankle. Even through her somewhat mangled hose, the swelling and discoloration were obvious. When she very gingerly moved it, the pain was hot and swift, but at least she *could* move it, so nothing was permanently harmed. Her head was clear once more, and she wasn't so queasy now, which was definitely a relief.

When Quinn returned to the room, he had her ice bag in one hand and a coffee cup in the other. "You left the coffee on," he told her as he handed the cup to her.

"I was in a temper," she admitted, avoiding his

eyes. Her voice was her own again, another thing to be thankful for, since she hated sounding like a wimp.

Without commenting on what she said, he got one of the decorative pillows from the other end of the couch and gently lifted her leg so that her foot and ankle were propped up. He eased the ice bag down on her swollen ankle, then left the room again, but only long enough to get a second cup of coffee from the kitchen.

When he came back, he startled her by sitting on the edge of the cushion at her thigh so that they were facing each other. He was sort of leaning sideways over her legs, one elbow and forearm resting on the back of the couch—either deliberately or accidentally blocking her in. The pressure of his hip against her leg distracted her from the heavenly relief of the ice bag on her ankle, and she wondered a bit wildly what spell he had used to make her body respond to him with such instant hunger.

Quinn took a sip of his coffee, then set the cup on the table and looked at her with those veiled eyes. In a carefully measured tone, he said, "Do you mind telling me what the hell you were doing out there tonight? And do you realize how close you came to getting yourself killed?"

"That wasn't the plan."

"Oh, you had a plan?"

"Don't be sarcastic, Alex—it doesn't suit you."

"And lying in a crumpled heap on a fire escape doesn't suit you." His voice was losing its measured precision; it was rougher now, harder. "What made you do it, Morgana? Why the hell were you on that fire escape?"

"I was looking for you, obviously. I don't know anyone else who might be found on the roof of a deserted building in the middle of the night."

Quinn refused to recognize her stab at self-mocking humor. "Why were you looking for me? Because I didn't come to the museum today?"

"No, of course not."

"Then why?"

"I told you, I was in a temper."

"About what?"

"About you!"

He frowned. "About me? Why? What had I done?"

Morgan took refuge in her coffee. She couldn't hide, but at least sipping it gave her a moment to think. Not that it helped; when she answered him, the words were blurted out with little grace and far too much pain.

"You swore you wouldn't use me again. You said you couldn't promise you wouldn't lie to me, but you *swore* you wouldn't try to use me or—or whatever's between us—for your own ends. And that's nearly a direct quote, dammit."

He was still frowning at her. "Morgana, I haven't tried to use you."

"Oh, no? Can you look me in the eye and tell me you haven't been very deliberately distracting me since the night at Leo's party when you went public as Alex Brandon? That you haven't used your Alex persona— all charm and seduction—to make sure I didn't ask too many questions about what Quinn was up to every night?"

"You talk as if I'm two men." His tone was odd, almost hesitant.

"You as good as say you are," she retorted instantly. "With some nice, neat dividing line separating you two. Night and day, black and white, Quinn and Alex. Two distinctly different men. Except that it's not that simple. You don't have a split personality, and you *aren't* two men. What you are is a hell of a natural actor."

"Am I?"

She nodded. "Oh, yes. A gifted one. Do you want me to tell you how I think your reasoning went?"

"Go ahead." His voice was a bit wry.

"I sat here for hours tonight thinking about it, trying to understand what you were doing and why you were making me feel so confused and out of control— and I finally got it."

He waited, silent and expressionless, his gaze fixed on her face.

"I think that when you decided to go public, there was one small problem you really hadn't planned on. Me." She held his gaze, determined to get this out. "There was something between us, something you couldn't ignore. Something real."

Quinn might have heard the very faint question there; he nodded and said gravely, "Yes. There was."

Morgan tried not to let her relief show; she'd been almost sure he hadn't been pretending a desire he hadn't felt. Almost. Going on steadily, she said, "Because of that, because you knew we'd be together often, you were afraid I'd figure out some things you didn't want me to know. For whatever reason."

"For your own good, maybe?" he suggested, more or less telling her she was on the right track.

"We'll talk about *that* later," she told him, ruthlessly keeping them on the subject. "The point is, you decided it would be a good idea to keep me distracted so I wouldn't think too much about the part Quinn was playing at night. So, being such an excellent actor, you turned Alex into an irresistible lover."

"Not quite," he murmured.

"That," she said, letting various kinds of frustration show through, "was part of the plan. And though I can forgive a lot, I'm not sure I'll ever forgive you for that."

"Morgana—"

"Wait. The defense can argue later."

He smiled slightly and nodded.

Morgan sighed. "Maybe you honestly don't think of it as using me and what I feel, but that's what you've been doing. I don't know if the reasons matter. I don't know if your reasons are good enough to excuse what you did. All I do know is that you used my feelings to help you hide what you were really doing here."

"What I'm *really* doing?"

"You said something once—that there were times you had to lie to everyone. This is one of those times, I think. All this isn't nearly as straightforward as you'd have us believe, this clever plan to catch Nightshade. You've been lying about it somehow. Maybe to Jared, probably to Max and Wolfe—and certainly to me."

"You think I'm after the collection," he said flatly.

"No."

"No?"

She smiled faintly at his disbelief. "No. Despite everything, including my own common sense, I don't believe you are. I can't know for certain what it is you're trying to do and how you're trying to do it—but I'm willing to bet the ultimate aim *is* to get Nightshade. It's in your voice every time you talk about him. You *do* really want him, and very badly, I think. So much so that you aren't going to let anyone or anything get in the way of catching him."

"That's what you think?"

"That's what I *feel*. Maybe Interpol thought you could catch Nightshade, but that isn't why you're here. You may be dancing to their tune, but only because it's your choice. And nobody's pulling your strings, Alex. Nobody. This—all this, this whole plan to set a trap—was your idea, wasn't it?"

Quinn stared at her for a long moment, then drew a breath and let it out slowly. "You think too much," he murmured, then smiled and added, "And you think too well."

"I'm right about this."

He hesitated, then nodded just a little. "The trap was my idea. Jared wasn't happy about it, but the chance to catch Nightshade was something he couldn't pass up. His . . . superiors at Interpol don't know what we're doing here."

That was a surprise, and Morgan knew it showed. "They don't know? You mean all this is unofficial?"

Quinn rubbed the back of his neck with one hand and looked at her wryly. "Morgana, Interpol doesn't have a policy of baiting traps with priceless gem collections. In fact, both Jared and I would likely land in jail if it got out that's what we're doing. Unless we're successful, of course. Because if we're successful, no one, except those of us directly involved, will ever know it was a trap."

"If Interpol doesn't know what you're doing, how is it that you're on the loose? I mean—"

"I know what you mean. Let's just say . . . Jared gambled on his little brother. His superiors believe he's over here on leave doing some consulting work—and I'm here to lend my own brand of expertise. Jared's responsible for me."

Morgan eyed him thoughtfully. "I got the impression that you two were barely on speaking terms. I gather it was a deliberate impression?"

Quinn had the grace to look a little sheepish. "I told you that a lot of what I do is pretense. Jared really *is* mad at me about half the time—he thinks I'm reckless and take too many dumb chances."

"You don't say."

"Sarcasm doesn't suit you either, Morgana."

She frowned at him. "Um. So you're the one who went to Max and asked him to risk his collection."

"I'm the one."

"Well, I must say I'm impressed. I knew he'd climb out on a fairly long limb for a friend, but you must be something pretty special."

He assumed a hurt expression. "You don't think so?"

"Stop that. You know what I mean."

Quinn smiled. "Yes, I know. And the truth is . . . Max and I go way back. Besides, once he heard about Nightshade's past activities, he thought catching the bastard sounded like an excellent idea."

Morgan was still frowning. She was reasonably sure that Quinn was being honest with her now, but that didn't mean he'd told her everything. He had an uncanny ability to tell just enough of the truth to make it all sound *right* without giving away anything he really didn't want someone else to know.

It was an unsettling talent—and it didn't help her to understand him the way she needed to. The problem was, she had yet to figure out what drove this man, what made him who he was. Everyone had some core motivation, some inner force propelling them through life as it shaped decisions and choices; what was his? She thought everything would make sense if she could only figure out what it was.

Slowly, probing for the answer to that question, she

said, "I think I said once that I thought you had a personal reason for going after Nightshade. Now I'm sure. And it isn't because he shot you. Why, Alex? What did he do to make you so determined? How did his path cross yours?"

Quinn didn't say a word for a moment. His face was still, wiped clean of all expression, and when he spoke, his voice was low and strained. "Two years ago, Nightshade killed someone who just happened to be in the wrong place at the wrong time—a not uncommon occurrence during one of his robberies. Only this time his victim was someone I cared about."

"Who?"

"Her name was Joanne. Joanne Brent. She was attending a party at a house in London and, apparently, wandered into her host's library looking for something to read. She surprised Nightshade at work—and he killed her. Left a dead rose on her body."

"That's awful," Morgan whispered.

"Yes." His voice was stony. "She was twenty-two."

Morgan searched his hard, handsome features, suddenly afraid of a ghost. "You . . . loved her." It wasn't a question.

He shook his head slightly, that look of rigid control softening a bit. "Not the way you mean. I never had a sister, but Joanne was the nearest thing. Until I came here to the States to attend college, we lived near each other in England. She was still a kid when I graduated—eight years younger—and after that I traveled quite a bit, so we didn't see each other often.

When she was killed, I hadn't seen her in nearly six months."

"Did she know you were Quinn?"

"No. I trusted her, but . . ."

Morgan said, "You didn't tell her because she would have worried?"

"Something like that."

After a moment Morgan nodded and said slowly, "You don't need me to point out that revenge tends to punish the one looking for it more than the target."

Quinn smiled, but his eyes were suddenly as hard and cold as emeralds. "I don't want revenge, Morgana. I want justice."

"What kind of justice?"

"The best kind. A man like Nightshade has spent his life collecting beautiful things, most of which he's secreted away so that his are the only eyes to see them. He sits in the middle of his treasures and gloats because he owns what no other man can claim." Quinn smiled again. "So I'm going to take all that away from him. I'm going to put him in jail, surrounded by bare concrete walls and men who have very little appreciation for beauty. And I'm going to make damned sure he rots there."

Morgan couldn't help shivering a little, but she tried to lighten the moment. "Sounds like a plan."

He looked hard at her for a moment, then smiled a much more genuine smile. "So it does."

She glanced down at the coffee cup she was cradling between her hands, absently aware that it was cooling, then returned her gaze to his face. "Your plan. You decided you could catch Nightshade, and you talked everybody else—Jared, Max, and Wolfe—into going along."

Thoughtfully, Quinn said, "I think Max convinced Wolfe. I was never very good with him. We always had . . . communications problems."

"He doesn't like thieves," Morgan reminded dryly.

"There is that, of course. And he's a bit hidebound about people who bend the law now and then. I always thought Max was as well, but he surprised me."

"You," Morgan said, "are a dangerous man. You have this weird ability to say the most outrageous things and make them sound perfectly reasonable."

Solemnly, Quinn said, "A certain inborn talent and a hell of a lot of practice."

"Umm. That isn't your only talent."

He cleared his throat. "I gather it's now the defense's turn to argue that point you mentioned earlier?"

"Well, if you thought you were going to get out of here without explaining it to me, think again." Morgan kept her voice light, but she was honestly upset and both of them knew it. He had deliberately used her desire for him to keep her off balance and distracted, and she really wasn't sure she would be able to forgive him for it.

Before he could begin, however, she went on matter-of-factly, "But I need to be clearheaded when I

DON'T HOLD BACK!

1. **No obligation!** No purchase necessary! Enter our Sweepstakes for a chance to win!
2. **FREE!** Get your first shipment of 6 Loveswept books, *and* a lighted makeup case as a free gift.
3. **Save money!** Become a member and about once a month you get 6 books for the price of 4! Return any shipment you don't want.
4. **Be the first!** You'll always receive your Loveswept books before they are available in stores. You'll be the first to thrill to these exciting new stories.

WINNERS CLASSIC SWEEPSTAKES
Entry Form

YES! I want to see where passion will lead me!

Place
FREE
ENTRY
Sticker
Here

Place
FREE
BOOKS
Sticker
Here

Enter me in the sweepstakes! I have placed my **FREE ENTRY** sticker on the heart.

Send me six *free* Loveswept novels *and* my *free* lighted makeup case! I have placed my **FREE BOOKS** sticker on the heart.

Mend a broken heart. Use both stickers to get the most from this special offer!

61234

NAME_____

ADDRESS_____ APT_____

CITY_____

STATE_____ ZIP_____

Loveswept's Heartfelt Promise to You!

There's no purchase necessary to enter the sweepstakes. There is no obligation to buy when you send for your 6 free books and free lighted makeup case. You may preview each new shipment for 15 days risk-free. If you decide against it, simply return the shipment within 15 days and owe nothing. If you keep the books, pay only $2.25 per book — a savings of $1.25 per book (plus postage & handling, and sales tax in NY and Canada). Prices subject to change. Orders subject to approval. See complete sweepstakes rules at the back of this book.

CD12

Give in to love and see where passion leads you!
Enter the Winners Classic Sweepstakes and
send for your **FREE** lighted makeup case and
6 **FREE** Loveswept books today!

(See details inside.)

listen, which demands a hot shower to wash away the last effects of the chloroform. What time is it?"

"Around one-thirty."

She held his gaze steadily. "Since you would have been up all night anyway, and since I'm wide-awake, I think tonight's a good time to settle this. Don't you?"

If he hesitated, it was only for an instant. "Yeah. So I'll make a fresh pot of coffee while you take your shower."

He took her cup and set it on the coffee table, then got to his feet. "How's the ankle?"

"Ask me when I'm standing."

Quinn helped her to her feet, keeping a firm grip on her arms until it became obvious that her injured ankle could bear weight, then he released her—but remained watchful.

Morgan hobbled toward her bedroom, relieved to find that the pain wasn't as bad as it had been. Over her shoulder to him, she said, "Back in a few minutes."

"I'll be here," he replied.

About that at least, she knew he was telling the truth.

SIX

By the time Morgan returned to the living room a little more than a quarter of an hour later, she felt much better physically. She'd washed away the grime of the fire escape and the memory of chloroform, carefully rubbed liniment on her sore ankle (the skin wasn't broken, but there was a nasty bruise), and thought about all he'd told her tonight.

The only certainty she had reached when she returned to him was the rueful knowledge that she had fallen for an extremely complex man she might never fully understand even after a lifetime of knowing him. On the other hand, he was also the most intriguing, baffling, maddening, exciting man she'd ever known, and impossibly sexy to boot.

None of that was a revelation, of course, except for her acceptance of her own feelings. And, being Morgan, once she accepted them, that particular struggle was over. After all, what was the use of kicking and screaming about something beyond one's power to change? She might be the last woman in the world who should have fallen in love with a famous cat burglar, but the fact remained that she *had*.

Dealing with it was the issue now.

After careful thought, Morgan very deliberately dressed in a loose and comfortable outfit consisting of baggy sweatpants and sweatshirt, with her only pair of bedroom slippers (ridiculously fuzzy things) on her feet. Hardly sexy attire. She had no intention of throwing herself at him yet again, and trusted that he would get the point.

Being Quinn, of course, he did.

"Where did you get the blanket?" she asked calmly as she limped back into the living room. The blanket had been folded up and placed over the back of a chair, catching her attention when she came in.

He had been on the couch looking rather broodingly at an old black-and-white movie on television, and got to his feet as soon as she spoke. His gaze scanned her from head to toe, and a faint gleam was born in the green eyes.

"Jared brought it when I called him to come relieve me on watch," he answered, then further explained by adding, "We have a cellular phone in case of emergencies."

"Ah. I wondered."

"Feeling better?"

"Heaps. Don't I look it?"

"Fishing, Morgana?"

"Curious."

He smiled. "I get the point, if that's what you're wondering. But I think I should tell you that you'd look sexy draped in sackcloth."

She eased down on the other end of the couch and looked up at him expressionlessly. "I always wondered what that was. Sackcloth, I mean."

"A very rough, coarse cloth."

"That was what I thought. But I wasn't sure. Did you happen to earn a college degree in the history of fashion?"

"No."

Morgan waited, one eyebrow rising, and Quinn suddenly uttered a low laugh.

"Actually, I have a law degree."

For an instant she wanted to laugh, but managed to control the impulse. "I see. Well, at least you completely understood the laws you were breaking."

"I'll get the coffee," Quinn said, retreating.

Morgan smiled to herself, then searched among the pillows on the couch for the remote and turned the television off. When he returned, she accepted her cup and sipped the hot liquid cautiously. "I won't be worth shooting tomorrow," she commented as he sat down a foot from her.

"You mean today." He glanced at her, then said, "I . . . called Jared while you were in the shower, and asked him to fill in the others in the morning. So they probably won't expect you to show up on time. If at all."

"I guess they had to know, huh?"

"I think so." Quinn gazed into his coffee cup as if it held the secrets of the universe. "If that *was* Nightshade who put you to sleep, he's getting either nervous or suspicious—and either could mean it's likely that he'll make his move soon."

There were still several questions Morgan wanted to ask about all this—things that bothered her in a sort of vague, indeterminate way—but she chose not to ask them right now for two reasons. First, because she was more than ready to focus on their relationship and, second, because she had a hunch he would tell her more if allowed to do so in his own way.

While all that was floating through her mind, he leaned forward to set his cup on the coffee table and then half turned toward her as he sat back.

"Morgana?"

She looked at him, finding his expression very serious.

"You're really angry with me, aren't you?"

"Furious," she confirmed quietly.

"I never meant to hurt you."

"No? How did you think I'd feel when—if—I realized what you were doing? Didn't it cross your mind that I might be just a tad upset once I understood that all this time while you've been talking about winning my trust, you've been deliberately and cold-bloodedly pushing all the right buttons?"

"That is not what happened," he protested instantly and in a very definite tone. "Maybe I did deliberately set out to make you want me—I seem to remember I told you as much—but there was nothing in the least cold-blooded about it. Trust me on that. I've lost ten pounds, uncounted hours of sleep—and yesterday I found my first gray hair."

"You were trying to distract me," she insisted, determined not to let him do that now.

"That was part of the reason, yes—I admit that. There were things I didn't want to have to explain—not yet anyway—and I knew damned well that if you concentrated that sharp mind of yours on what I was doing at night, you'd figure out more than I wanted you to know."

"Thanks for the compliment," she said dryly. "But I've a feeling your little plan is so twisty I wouldn't be able to find my way through it with a road map."

He smiled slightly. "Maybe not. I think I've taken a few turns blindly myself. That happens when you have to improvise without warning."

"We're straying from the point," she said in the most severe tone she could manage. "Which is—"

"I know what it is." He sighed. "I'm just trying to avoid it."

His honesty was rather disarming, but Morgan stuck to her guns. "Why?"

Quinn reached over and got her coffee cup, setting it beside his, then took both her hands and held them firmly. "Morgana, you were right when you said I hadn't planned on you. I hadn't. You were . . . unexpected in more ways than one. But I thought I could deal with it. I thought I could handle how I felt about you without letting it distract me too much from what I had to do. At first. Then when I came to you after I was shot, not out of reason or logic, but just because . . . because I had an overwhelming need to be with you, I knew I was in trouble. And I knew I didn't have a hope in hell of keeping you in a nice, safe little compartment of my life—even to protect you."

Morgan resisted the urge to ask him to define his feelings for her a bit more clearly; she was determined not to prod him to say anything he wasn't ready to divulge on his own. "Protect me from what?"

"From all the risks involved in what I'm doing." He sounded frustrated. "Dammit, Nightshade *kills* people, don't you understand that? Without a second thought or even an instant's hesitation, he kills anyone who gets in his way. I don't want you in his way, Morgana. I don't want him to even imagine you could be a problem. It's bad enough that you're publicly linked with me at all; the closer you are to me, the closer you are to *him*—visible to him and drawing his attention. Besides that, considering how many times you had already charged into dangerous situations—"

"Just that one time, when I followed those men who had you," she objected. "You can't count the first time, because I was there by accident; my date took me to that museum in all innocence." Then she frowned.

"Well, maybe not innocence—but you know what I mean."

"What about tonight?"

"That hadn't happened yet, so don't use it as an excuse."

He almost laughed, making a sound that was actually more of despair.

"All right, but even then it's been obvious all along that you're too impulsive for your own good. And I could hardly count on *my* good sense where you're concerned; I knew that I wouldn't be able to stay away from you. Seeing you openly as Alex Brandon seemed the best way. But it meant Nightshade would have to know I was interested in you, and his awareness of that was enough of a risk. I didn't want you getting involved with my—my nighttime activities. So I thought that both being Alex during the day and conducting a fairly normal courtship would make you seem unthreatening to Nightshade and distract your attention from what I was doing at night."

Morgan blinked. There were several things bothering her about all that, but one realization was uppermost in her mind. "Wait a minute. Are you saying that you went public just because of me? It wasn't part of your plan to find Nightshade?"

"I'd already found Nightshade," he admitted reluctantly. "And for God's sake, don't tell Jared—he'd shoot me."

She felt a bit dazed. "You had already found Nightshade. And being Alex won't help lure him into the trap?"

"As a matter of fact, being Alex was one of those improvised turns I mentioned—and it's complicated the situation in more ways than I want to discuss."

Morgan stared at him. Almost idly, she said, "You know, if I find out your name isn't really Alex, I'll—"

He didn't wait to hear what she'd do. "I give you my word of honor that my mother named me Alexander. Satisfied?"

"On that point. But I'm very puzzled about the rest of this," she admitted. "And I've got this weird feeling that you've distracted me again."

Gravely, he said, "We always seem to cover a remarkable amount of ground when we talk, don't we? But I believe your original question concerned my reprehensible behavior in . . . making you want me?"

She shook her head.

"Trying to distract you by making you want me?"

"Partly that. It *was* reprehensible of you."

"I know. I'm sorry."

Morgan struggled silently, but finally gave in and said, "It's not just what you did—it's the way you did it. Do you know I made an absolute fool of myself at work today—I mean yesterday? You had me so crazy, I hardly knew what I was doing. But everybody else recognized what was wrong with me. Easily. I wasn't just wearing my heart on my sleeve, I had a damned *billboard* hovering over my head."

Quinn's hands tightened on hers, but his face remained grave. "I didn't realize I had such a powerful effect on you."

She eyed him with a healthy amount of bitter resentment. "Oh, yes, you did. You aren't blind or stupid, and I was about as subtle as neon. But what I'm really having a hard time forgiving is your cruelty."

"My—"

"Yes, your cruelty!" She glared at him. "Why the hell did you pick *that* way to distract me when—when you had no intention of following through?"

After a moment he said slowly, "Morgana, what I told you at Leo's party was the truth. Without trust between lovers—"

She was incredulous. "Trust? Alex, stop and think a minute. I am a sensible, rational, law-abiding woman who never so much as cheated on a parking meter before I met you. So what happened the night we met? I lied to the police when I didn't tell them you stole that dagger. And what happened the night those thugs grabbed you? Not only did I risk life and limb to try to help you, but then I more or less betrayed my good friend and employer, Max—I thought—by warning you that Mysteries Past was a trap. And I didn't call the cops when you lay bleeding on my floor. Does any of this suggest something to you? Like maybe that I seem to have a certain lack of good judgment where you're concerned?"

His eyes were even more vivid than usual, and his mouth curved in a slight smile. "But do you trust me?"

Morgan sighed and abandoned her last shred of dignity. "I love you, and that'll have to be good enough."

She had the satisfaction of knowing she had surprised him, at least, but she couldn't read anything else in his suddenly still face and brilliant eyes.

"Say that again," he murmured.

"I love you." She said it quietly and without drama, but with utter certainty. "I've known that for weeks."

Quinn leaned forward slowly, releasing her hands so that his arms could encircle her, pulling her toward him as his head bent and his warm, hard mouth found hers. Morgan made a little sound, much as she had when he'd picked her up, and her arms slid up around his neck eagerly. She could no more temper her instant, fiery response to him than she could stop the runaway beating of her heart.

Her body seemed attuned to him, to his touch, in a way she'd never felt before. It was nothing so simple as passion; what he ignited in her was a craving so elemental and absolute, it was akin to the need of her body for sustenance. She had the dim realization that some part of her would starve to death without him.

He lifted his head at last and looked at her with eyes so dark there was only a hint of green visible. Huskily, he said, "I promised myself I wouldn't let anything . . . irrevocable happen between us until I could be completely honest with you. Until you could know the truth. Morgana—"

She slid her fingers into his thick silvery hair and

pulled him down so that she could kiss him. Against his mouth she murmured, "Alex, I want you . . . and that's the only truth I care about right now."

Quinn hesitated for another moment, his entire body tense, but then he made a rough sound and kissed her hungrily. His hands moved down her back, probing through the material of her sweatshirt, while the tip of his tongue teased the sensitive inner surface of her lips. Morgan heard herself utter another of those primitive little whimpers, wordless but urgent with wanting, and then all her senses went haywire at the stark, carnal possession of his tongue.

Just like before, the relentless need Morgan felt for him was stunning—but this time she was aware that he was every bit as involved in what was happening as she was. He wasn't holding back, wasn't detached, and wasn't trying to distract her. And he didn't have to try to make her want him.

Morgan hadn't intended this to happen tonight, she really hadn't, but the only emotional hesitation she felt about it was a need to be reassured that he wouldn't walk away from her as he had before. "Stay with me," she invited unsteadily when his lips trailed across her cheek and traced her jawline. "Stay with me tonight."

"Are you sure, sweetheart?" he demanded hoarsely, drawing away just far enough to make her look at him. His handsome face was taut, his features drawn with a sharpened look of hunger. "I didn't come here prepared for this."

She understood what he was saying, but since she'd

never been able to be practical about him anyway, Morgan didn't see any reason to break with tradition at this late date. "I'm sure. I want you to stay."

Quinn looked at her for a moment longer, then kissed her again, more deeply still, almost as if that alone were an act of possession. It sent her senses spinning, stealing her breath and increasing the feverish heat of her desire until Morgan wasn't thinking about anything except how he made her feel. Then he was shifting his hold on her, lifting her, and she realized he was carrying her as easily as he had before.

Since he'd spent several days there, he was familiar with her apartment, and was able to find his way to her bedroom almost blindly. She had left the lamp on her nightstand on, so soft light illuminated the room, and she blinked up at him a bit dazedly when he set her on her feet beside the bed.

He framed her face in his hands and looked down at her with an odd intensity, as if memorizing her features, his own still strained. "That first night in the museum," he murmured, "when you looked up at me with your cat's eyes, so indignant to find yourself in the company of a thief, I knew this would happen. Even then, I knew."

She managed a smile. "All I knew was how much you annoyed me. And how empty that room seemed when you left."

His thumb brushed her bottom lip in a rhythmic little caress. "I didn't go far that night. I watched the police come, and when they brought you back here, I followed them."

"You did?"

"Mmm. And I was at the museum during the day a couple of times after that. So I could see you."

"Before I knew what you looked like . . . but I had a feeling you were somewhere around."

He uttered a low sound that was almost a laugh, then kissed her, the first light touch deepening rapidly.

Morgan touched his chest, probing through his black sweater to feel the hardness of muscle and bone. The faint musky scent of his body was familiar to her and wildly arousing, and the touch of his hands and lips, the touch of *him*, only fed her hunger. In that moment she was peculiarly conscious of being female in a way that was totally new to her.

She pushed the hem of his sweater up blindly because she had to touch his skin, half opening her eyes when he let go of her long enough to yank the garment off and toss it aside. Her eyes went immediately to his left shoulder, and her fingers gently touched the scar there. He'd been right, she realized; he did heal quickly. It was difficult to believe he'd been shot hardly more than three weeks ago.

But the scar *was* a reminder, a sign of the danger of what he was doing, and that was something Morgan didn't want to think about right now. She pressed her lips to the puckered skin, her fingers exploring his ribs, then sliding up his hard body to stroke the thick golden hair covering his chest. It was a sensual delight to touch him, but she wanted more, much more—and Quinn seemed to feel the same.

He pulled her sweatshirt off almost roughly, then sat down on the edge of the bed and, his hands at her small waist, pulled her a step closer so that she was standing between his knees. His mouth feathered over her breastbone, then slowly brushed her skin above the lace edging of her bra.

Morgan was holding his shoulders for support because she wasn't sure how much longer her legs would hold her up; she thought all her bones were melting. His hands slid up her sides slowly, then moved to cup her breasts very gently, the touch so light that it was maddening. His lips trailed almost lazily over the upper slope of one breast, then his tongue lightly traced the valley between them.

She shivered in an instant, heated response, her back arching of its own volition and her nails digging into his shoulders. Her beasts felt hot and swollen, aching, and she thought she'd die if he didn't strip away the material covering them and touch her bare flesh. "Alex . . ." she murmured unsteadily.

He might have heard the plea in her voice, or he might have given in to his own impatience, but in any case his long, clever fingers coped swiftly with the back clasp of her bra. Morgan was only dimly aware of freeing her arms from the straps, but she caught her breath when she realized the bra was gone and that she was naked to the waist.

During Morgan's months-long relationship with

her fiancé during college, she had always been self-conscious about her centerfold measurements, and she'd never felt much when her breasts were touched or caressed. But now, when Quinn's hands touched her and his lips slid over her hot flesh toward a tingling nipple, the tense, burning pleasure was so powerful she bit her lip to keep from crying out.

Then she did cry out, stunned by the wash of sensations when he captured her nipple. The strong suction of his warm mouth and his teasing, fluttering tongue combined to drive her to the edge of madness. All the remaining strength drained from her legs in a rush and she sagged against him, boneless. He held her easily, turning her slightly so that she was half sitting on his thigh, while he caressed her breasts.

There was a moment when Morgan decided, with absolute clarity, that Quinn really did want to drive her mad, but before she could find the breath to cuss at him for it, he was lifting her and then placing her in the center of the bed. She wouldn't have let go of him on her own; he gently unlocked her fingers from the back of his neck once she was on the bed, and the only reason she allowed it was because it was obvious he had no intention of leaving her there alone.

He got rid of his boots and socks quickly, then bent over the bed to ease off Morgan's slippers. Her fuzzy slippers. She heard him utter a soft laugh as he took them off, and even in her dazed condition she was aware of a wry realization.

"Not very sexy," she murmured, speaking aloud before she could stop herself.

"No," he agreed huskily. "But perfect."

She wanted to ask him to explain that comment, but he was kissing her and his hands were stripping her sweatpants and panties down her legs, and she more or less forgot. Then he was with her again, the remainder of his clothing discarded, and Morgan moaned when his mouth returned to her breasts. His teeth raked gently over her tightly beaded flesh, his tongue soothed, and his hands kneaded with a sure, sensitive touch.

Burning, so tense she thought she might explode, Morgan explored his shoulders and back with trembling fingers and tried to be still. But her body wanted to move, had to move, and she couldn't seem to stop the wordless sounds that kept welling up from deep inside her.

He stroked her quivering belly, his hand moving slowly downward, and she felt her legs part for him. He touched her mound gently, fingers sliding into the black curls, probing until they found slick heat and throbbing need. Sensations raced along her nerve endings, hot and intense, and she couldn't breathe, couldn't plead with him to stop or not to stop, couldn't do anything except endure the scalding wash of feelings.

Just when Morgan knew she couldn't bear it a moment longer, when she was sure her body would shatter, Quinn opened her legs and slipped between them. She gasped when she felt the smooth hardness of him part her slippery flesh, felt the slow but inexorable penetration. It had been a long time for her, but even so she would have sworn she had never felt this before, this stark intimacy and primitive sense of joining.

His face above her was hard, the burning eyes fierce with need, his breathing as ragged as hers. That was all Morgan saw before he began moving inside her—and she was swept along on a rising tide of rapture. He sent her out of control yet again, but this time she gloried in the freedom of it. Her body, so finely attuned to him, responded to his passion and her own as if they had been meant to be lovers for all time.

The relentless intensity of that passion built until Morgan was . . . almost . . . afraid of what was happening to her. But by then it was too late, far too late, and she cried out wildly when the intensity reached a shattering peak. Waves of pleasure washed over her, through her. . . . She was dimly aware of his hoarse sound of release, of his marvelous heavy body settling on her, and she wanted to never have to move again.

Morgan made a soft, disgruntled sound when he jostled her a bit while he was getting them under the covers, but she didn't open her eyes even when he chuckled. She felt utterly limp and sated, and as he pulled her close to his side again once they were both under the covers, she pillowed her head on his shoulder with a sigh of pure bliss.

"Morgana?"

"Hmm?"

"Am I forgiven?"

She still didn't want to open her eyes, though she was very much awake. After a moment she said, "Don't spread the word around, but I can't stay mad at you no matter what you do."

His arm tightened around her, and one hand began smoothing her long hair. "I know you aren't still mad—but am I forgiven?"

Morgan lifted her head then and looked down at him. He was serious, she realized. She pushed herself up on one elbow to see him better, and answered seriously. "You're forgiven. But don't ever do that to me again, Alex. I think I can stand being lied to easier than being manipulated."

He was still toying with her hair, and a slight frown drew his brows together. Softly, he said, "I don't want to lie to you."

"No—but you aren't ready to tell me the truth." She gave him a rueful smile.

"I have my reasons, sweetheart. I think they're good reasons. Can you accept that?"

She hesitated. "I want to. But it's driving me crazy wondering how many lies you've told me. Can you at least promise that you'll tell me the truth eventually?"

Quinn nodded immediately. "Once the trap is sprung, I swear I'll tell you everything."

"Then I'll accept that." She kept her voice light. "Just . . . don't lie about this, all right? About us. I don't want any bedroom promises, Alex."

His hand slid to the nape of her neck, and he pulled her down and kissed her slowly. Against her mouth, he murmured, "No bedroom promises."

Morgan had thought herself exhausted, but as his warm mouth moved against hers she felt a surge of energy . . . and desire. Quinn seemed equally refreshed; his kisses deepened into hunger, and then he was pressing her against the pillows and pushing the covers back so he could see her.

For a moment—even after all that had gone before—Morgan felt a little shy. The way he was looking at her, so direct and intent, was a bit unnerving. But then he leaned down to press a soft kiss on her stomach, then another and another in a slow trail up between her breasts, and his low words added a sensual vibration and another kind of seduction to the caresses.

"No bedroom promises . . . just the truth. Have you any idea what you do to me? What you've been doing to me since the night I reached out and caught you? There hasn't been a day you haven't been on my mind, and the nights . . . the nights. The nights never seemed long before, but now they do, long and cold."

"Even this night?" she asked huskily.

"No." He lifted his head and looked down at her with darkening eyes. "Not this night."

Then he was moving, parting her legs and slipping

between them. She felt his burning flesh sink deeply into her body and gasped at the suddenness of the raw need he ignited in her. Her hands caught at his back, fingers digging in, and she moaned, her legs lifting to cradle him eagerly.

His forearms under her shoulders, he tangled his fingers in her hair and held her as if she were trying to escape him. His mouth covered hers, the kiss hot and hard, and his lower body barely moved.

Morgan had had no idea that she was even capable of such a swift and total response, but she soared toward the brink so quickly it was like yielding to an elemental force. He was inside her, filling her, and her newly awakened body was electrified by the sensations. She could feel the heavy ache of her breasts, the hard points of her nipples teased by the mat of hair covering his chest; her body was frantic to move.

"You're beautiful," he said huskily, his eyes narrowed on her taut face. "Especially like this, so alive, wanting me."

She couldn't have said anything to that if her life had depended on it. The coiling tension inside her held her in a blissful state of pleasure so acute it bordered on pain, and she couldn't even catch her breath enough to moan.

Quinn's eyes narrowed even more as he slowly, tortuously, began to move, subtle undulations becoming deep, lazy thrusts, and Morgan couldn't bear it another second. It felt as if every nerve ending she possessed throbbed in rhythmic surges of pleasure, and her wild cry was caught in his mouth as he kissed her fiercely.

He followed her over the brink, his powerful body shuddering and a hoarse sound wrenched from him, and this time, sated and utterly drained, they both slept.

The sky was just beginning to lighten toward gray when Quinn slipped from the bed, careful not to wake Morgan, and went to gaze out the bedroom window. As Morgan had noted, he was accustomed to working nights, and it had reached a point where he found it difficult to sleep when it was dark.

If this kept up much longer, he reflected wryly, he really *would* turn into a vampire.

He stood there at the window, looking out on the quiet street in front of the apartment building, acutely aware of the soft breathing of the woman in the bed behind him. How to keep her safe? That was his greatest worry now. He had tried not to let her see how shaken he had been over what had happened on the fire escape, but the truth was that every time he thought of the danger she'd been in it was like a knife in his heart.

And now what? He was running out of time, dammit, he could feel it. After tonight, he was going to be walking a high wire without a net, and he wasn't sure he could maintain his balance. Not now. Not anymore.

"Alex?"

He turned immediately, crossing the dim room to

return to the bed. Sliding under the covers, he pulled her into his arms and held her without force, fighting the instincts urging him to hold her with all his strength. "Sorry I woke you," he murmured.

"Is something wrong?" she asked softly, her warm body pressed to his.

"No, sweetheart, nothing's wrong," he lied. "Go back to sleep."

Within minutes she had, her breath soft against his skin. Very gently, careful not to wake her, he stroked her back, enjoying the satiny feel of her skin and the radiant warmth of her body.

She loved him. That was what she'd said, and said with quiet conviction. Knowing him for a liar and a thief, she loved him. It was remarkable. *She* was remarkable.

Staring up at the ceiling of her bedroom, Quinn wondered if Morgan would love him when she knew the truth.

SEVEN

The room was bright when Morgan finally opened her eyes, and for a moment she lay there on her stomach in the middle of the bed, just blinking drowsily, her body warm beneath the covers. She felt wonderful. Different, though. So relaxed and content she wanted to purr like a cat sprawled in the sunlight. Every inch of her skin seemed heated in a strange new way, and she had the odd notion that she could feel her heart beating throughout her entire body.

She didn't want to move, reluctant to do anything that might change the blissful sense of fulfillment she felt. But she wasn't a woman who could be still for long unless she was sleeping, and the drowsiness left her. Gradually, she focused on the clock on her nightstand. Twelve. Twelve noon.

Frowning, she pushed herself up onto her elbows, staring at the clock. Noon? She hadn't slept this late in years, why on earth would she— Then she remembered.

It all came back to her in a rush, and she twisted quickly to look around her bedroom, ignoring a few twinges from muscles protesting the sudden movement. The room was empty except for her. But . . . those clothes on the storage chest at the foot of her bed; weren't they his? Black sweater and pants, folded neatly . . . Yes, she thought they were his.

Morgan pushed herself upright and only then heard quiet music from the other side of the apartment. She didn't hear Quinn, but she was certain he was still here. She could feel his nearness, an odd inner certainty she had noticed before this. After a moment she slid to the edge of the bed, another twinge in her ankle reminding her of last night's injury. It didn't look too bad, she decided, just a bit puffy and wearing spectacular colors; when she stood up cautiously, it held her weight with only slight pain.

When she went into the bathroom, she realized Quinn had recently taken a shower; the air was still damp, and so was a towel he had draped over the shower-curtain rod. She thought he'd probably used the electric razor she had provided for him when he'd stayed here before.

She took her own shower, letting the hot water clear her mind even as it soothed her sore body. She'd noticed a few more faint bruises that had resulted from her struggle on the fire escape, and between that and her unusually active night, she was definitely a little stiff.

The hot water certainly helped, so she lingered there, washing her hair and smiling to herself when she remembered his fingers tangled in it. When she finally got out of the tub and wrapped her hair in a towel, she still felt a bit stiff but much better. She rummaged in the vanity cabinets underneath the sink and found a bottle of body lotion in the scent of the perfume she usually wore, and rubbed some of it into her skin. She knew it was the rubbing rather than the lotion that made her muscles feel looser and less strained—but soft, scented skin was an added benefit that any woman with a lover could easily appreciate.

Morgan wrapped a towel around herself and began drying her hair, and as her blow dryer roared she thought about that. A lover. Was that what Quinn would be? She didn't know, she really didn't. The timing of all this, considering the circumstances, was hardly the best, and even if it had been, Quinn was not what anyone would choose to call predictable.

Or conventional. Given who and what he was, it was entirely possible that this interlude with her was no more than that—a respite in the middle of a tense situation to let him unwind and seek a purely sexual release of stress.

That was a depressing possibility, she decided, but one she had to consider at least logical and perhaps likely. He was, after all, an unusually handsome and charming man somewhere in his early thirties—and though the mysterious Quinn might not have wished to risk possible exposure of his identity with a sex life, his daytime persona of Alex had undoubtedly enjoyed the company of eager females over the years. The evidence of that was clear; he'd been a skilled and sensitive lover, and that required both experience and a thorough knowledge of a woman's body and what would please her.

Morgan was hardly shocked by these realizations. In fact, she wasn't particularly surprised by them. She was a rational woman, and she'd had weeks since meeting Quinn to consider the matter. She had, in fact, thought about him and what involvement with him might mean to the point that she was reasonably sure she had considered every possibility.

Not that it helped, really. It might have been possible in the last weeks to detach her emotions far enough to contemplate the possible consequences of taking a very famous and very enigmatic cat burglar into her bed, but once it had happened, her detachment was gone. Only emotions were left, and all those told her was what she *felt*. She loved him. Beyond reason or rationality, beyond common sense or consequences, she loved him.

And that was what she had to endure, no matter what the future brought.

By the time her hair was dry, Morgan had more or less decided to play this new turn in their relationship by ear. What other choice did she have? Her life was clearly defined and spread out before him; there were no mysteries, no hidden facts, no false names . . . no lies. Who and what she was was obvious to him. Who and what *he* was, on the other hand, was still somewhat nebulous. The only thing she knew for certain was that what he was doing was dangerous.

So at least until Quinn's trap for Nightshade was sprung, her instincts told her to accept whatever he offered and be as patient as she could. Once that was over and he could tell her the truth, then perhaps there would be a discussion about some kind of future for them. Or perhaps not.

Perhaps Quinn would return to Europe and the life he enjoyed and knew so well. Without her.

There was, in any case, absolutely nothing she could do either to make him love her or make him stay with her. She had a better chance of catching lightning in a bottle than she had of capturing him, and besides that, the last thing she would have chosen would be to see him trapped. Whatever he did in the end had to be his own decision, without pressure from her.

She returned to the bedroom, still thoughtful, and briefly debated before pulling a gold silk robe from her closet. It was one of those garments a single woman might buy for herself but then not wear simply because it was designed for a man to look at, something rich and elegant that caressed the body in a touch of pure sensuality.

Well, she acknowledged silently, there was pressure . . . and then there was *pressure*. After all, no female worth the gender would just stand by and let the man she loved make up his mind about things without reminding him of a few advantages a sensible and rational woman could provide. That was certainly fair.

Without vanity, Morgan knew she looked good in the deceptively simple robe. The color suited her, and the shimmering material clung to her body in all the right places. She couldn't help smiling a little as she tied the belt at her waist, remembering last night's sweatshirt and pants—and the fuzzy slippers. Talk about going from the ridiculous to the sublime!

Barefoot, she padded out into the living room. Empty, with music videos playing quietly on the television. She continued on to the kitchen, and there found Quinn, his back to her, busy preparing what looked like an appetizing brunch of pancakes with fruit. Since he'd helped in the kitchen while recovering from his wound, Morgan wasn't surprised by his skill. And he was wearing jeans and a white shirt, some of his own clothes that had been left behind here weeks ago.

She knew very well that his still being here today was a good sign (she had half expected him to leave before she awakened), but Morgan refused to let herself attach too much importance to that. *One step at a time, that's the way to go.*

"Hi," she greeted him casually.

He looked over his shoulder at her, mouth opening to say something that never got said. Instead, he stared at her for a moment, brilliant green eyes scanning her from bare toes to gleaming hair; then he turned a dial on the griddle, set the spatula on the counter beside it, and came to her.

Somewhat breathlessly, a few minutes later, she said, "I always forget how big you are until I'm standing close to you. Why is that?"

"I have no idea." He nuzzled the side of her neck, inhaling slowly. "You smell wonderful."

Her arms up around his neck—and her feet off the floor since he'd lifted her—Morgan murmured something wordless in response and wondered vaguely how his body could feel so hard and yet so pleasurable against hers. He had both his arms tightly wrapped around her, so that she was certain there wasn't a square inch of her front not pressed to his, and since her silk robe was whisper thin, it felt as though only the slight barrier of his clothing separated them.

Then he lifted his head suddenly and frowned, and Morgan felt herself being lowered back to her feet.

"I was enjoying myself," she protested.

He smiled slightly, but the frown remained in his eyes. One hand gently brushed her hair back away from her neck. "Sweetheart, did I do this?"

She didn't feel pain when he touched her very lightly just below her ear, but she knew he was looking at a faint bruise because she'd seen it in the mirror. "No, I think our friend on the fire escape did it. If he hadn't been wearing gloves, you could probably get his thumbprint off me. It was when he was holding that cloth over my face."

Quinn nodded slightly, an expression she couldn't

read flaring in his eyes. He lowered his head and kissed her briefly, though still as hungrily as before. "I heard the shower, so I thought you'd be ready for breakfast."

Morgan smiled at him. "I'm starving. But you turned the griddle up instead of down, and the pancakes are burning."

Swearing rather creatively, he released her and hastily went back to the counter to pry smoldering pancakes off the griddle. Morgan turned on the exhaust fan over the stove, hoping to avoid having the smoke detector outside her bedroom door go off, then opened the kitchen window for good measure. A cool breeze wafted in obediently, and the smoke was dissipated before it could do any harm.

"I'm glad I made extra batter," he commented ruefully as he dumped blackened pancakes into the trash can. "I must have known you'd come in here looking the way Helen of Troy must have looked when she launched all those ships."

"You sweet talker, you," Morgan said.

Stirring his batter, Quinn sent her a smile. "Tell me something, Morgana. Do you believe anything I say?"

"'Bout half," she conceded as she poured herself a cup of coffee. "I'd consider myself in serious need of therapy if I believed more than that."

He chuckled, but sent her another glance, this one more sober. "Regrets?"

Remembering what he'd said about what could happen if they became lovers without trust, she shook her head and smiled at him. "No, no regrets. I knew what I was doing."

For a moment he concentrated on his cooking, expertly flipping the golden pancakes. Then, softly, he said, "We were both reckless."

Having realized this discussion would take place, Morgan was ready for it and responded calmly. "If you mean birth control, it's all right. My doctor put me on the pill a couple of years ago for an irregular cycle."

He looked at her, very direct. "You don't have to worry about anything else."

"Neither do you." Leaning back against the counter, she conjured a rather regretful smile. "It's become a dangerous world, hasn't it?"

Quinn leaned over and kissed her, gently this time. "It always was, sweetheart. The only difference is that now the dangers aren't so obvious—and too often tend to be potentially fatal."

"Yeah. Sometimes it's the pits being a grown-up," Morgan observed. But then, since she was a naturally optimistic woman, her absent attention fixed on him as he turned the pancakes onto two plates, and her gaze wandered over his broad shoulders, down his back to his lean waist, and then to his narrow hips and long legs. He looked awfully good in jeans, she reflected. Only half-aware of making the sound, she sighed. "Then again . . . sometimes it's not bad at all."

Her thoughts must have been obvious from her voice, because he smiled without looking at her and murmured, "You're a wicked woman, Morgana."

Somewhat dryly, she said, "No, just human."
Then she refilled their coffee cups and helped him
transfer the food to her small kitchen table.

It wasn't until later, when they were finished with
the meal and had cleaned up the kitchen, that Morgan
somewhat cautiously turned their casual conversation
in a more serious direction. "Alex . . . you aren't
going to tell me who Nightshade is?"

He had followed her into the living room, and when
she asked the question he put his hands on her shoulders and turned her to face him. "We've talked about
this, Morgana. If you came face-to-face with a man you
knew was Nightshade, could you trust yourself not to
react to that knowledge?"

"I suppose not." She looked up at him steadily.
"But I would like to know how badly I screwed things
up by climbing that fire escape last night."

He didn't pretend to misunderstand. "Hardly at
all—*if* I can persuade Nightshade that you were going
up there to visit Alex Brandon, with no idea I'm also
Quinn."

"Why would I think I could find Alex on a rooftop
somewhere around midnight?" she asked dryly.

In a matching tone he said, "Help me think of a
reason, will you? The last thing I want is for Nightshade to start wondering if you know I'm Quinn. Because once he does that, he might also wonder why a
woman of well-known honesty and integrity such as
yourself would be keeping quiet about that."

"And smell a trap?"

"In his place, I would."

Morgan bit her bottom lip for a moment, then eased back away from him and went to sit down—in the chair rather than on the couch. She had trouble thinking clearly when he touched her, and she wanted to think about this.

Quinn sat down at the end of the couch nearest her chair, watching her gravely.

"Alex . . . *he* knows you're Quinn. I mean, he knows that Alex Brandon is Quinn." There was a faint question in her voice, even though she was sure she was right.

"He knows."

"Then I don't understand. He knows you're Quinn, and you know he's Nightshade . . . and you're both wanted by the police in several countries. You're both eyeing Mysteries Past because the Bannister collection is something any thief would want—and each of you knows about the other's interest in it. How does that add up to a trap?"

Quinn hesitated, then sighed. "Actually, it's more like a sting. You see, for reasons I'd rather not discuss, Nightshade can't go after the Bannister collection alone. He needs a partner—and I'm it."

Morgan opened her mouth, but then closed it. If Quinn said he'd "rather not" discuss something, then he wouldn't. So instead of asking about that, she merely said, "Okay. But why couldn't Quinn go after the collection alone? I mean, why would Quinn need Nightshade?"

"Several reasons," he answered willingly enough. "Because the States are . . . unfamiliar ground to Quinn, for one. Even a thief who apparently acts alone has to have contacts: inside sources or informants with reliable information, trustworthy people to provide supplies and equipment, some quick and safe means of transportation once the job is done. All my contacts are in Europe—and I'd have a hell of a time transporting the collection back there. But I came here anyway because, as you say, the Bannister collection is irresistible.

"So . . . when I stumble across another thief while casing the museum—and survive him shooting me—I make it a point to look him up once I've recovered. He's naturally upset that I was able to find him, but I make it clear I don't particularly care who he is and that I have no intention of horning in on his territory. No, I'm going to go back to Europe—but I want very badly to take one piece of the Bannister collection with me."

"The Bolling?" she guessed.

Quinn smiled slightly. "Are you kidding? That bloody thing's got a curse on it. Every time it's been stolen in its long and colorful history, it's brought disaster to the thief."

Startled, she said, "I didn't know that was the curse."

"Oh, yes, and it's well documented. The diamond came into the hands of the Bannisters somewhere around 1500—legitimately. A gentleman named Edward Bannister found the uncut and unpolished stone lying in a stream bed in India. Just lying right out in the open."

"Talk about luck," Morgan said.

"Yeah. Anyway, he had the stone polished—not faceted—and gave it as a betrothal present to his bride. The first attempt to steal it actually occurred during their honeymoon, and the would-be thief broke his neck trying to escape out a window. Rumor has it that Edward stood over the body wearing nothing but a sheet grabbed in haste from the connubial bed, and promptly declared to all present that the diamond was obviously fated to belong to his family and would henceforth be considered an amulet. Then he christened the stone the Bolling diamond."

"Why Bolling?"

Quinn smiled. "Well, Edward couldn't call it the Bannister diamond, because he already had one with that moniker. So he had to think of something else. And it seems he possessed a somewhat ironic sense of humor. The thief who broke his neck trying to steal the stone went by the name of Thomas Bolling."

"And the stone he couldn't steal would forever wear his name. That is ironic. And it's a strange kind of fame."

"Thomas Bolling would probably be pleased; from all accounts, he was both stupid and somewhat depraved, and likely would have passed through history unknown if not for his encounter with that pretty yellow diamond."

Morgan eyed Quinn. "Are you *sure* you aren't making this up? It spins very readily off your silver tongue."

"I swear. Ask Max."

"Umm. Okay, so then that happened?"

"Well, by uttering what he most likely thought would be a warning that would ward off superstitious thieves at least, old Edward appears to have laid a solid foundation for the curse. Maybe fate was listening. Or maybe there simply followed a very long string of amazingly unlucky thieves. In any case, the Bolling diamond began to build quite a reputation. In those days, the stone probably weighed at least a hundred carats and likely more, so it was quite a target. And later on, when it was faceted and eventually set into the pendant, it was so breathtaking that few could resist the lure of it.

"During the next four hundred years, there were dozens of attempts to steal it, some of them remarkably ingenious. But nobody could successfully get it away from the Bannister family. Without exception, all the thieves died—most in decidedly painful ways. A few were caught and died in prison, but all of them died because of that stone."

Morgan shivered a little. She wasn't a superstitious woman, but the story definitely unnerved her. No doubt because she was in love with a jewel thief. She cleared her throat and said a bit fiercely, "You stay away from that thing."

He smiled and moved suddenly, sliding off the couch and onto his knees in front of her chair. Before she could do anything, his hands were on her knees, easing them apart. She caught her breath as warm fingers stroked her outer thighs, then slip upward very slowly, under the silk of her robe, until they could cup her bottom and pull her toward him.

"I'm not going to steal the Bolling, Morgana," he murmured, his eyes heavy-lidded and intense. He kissed the side of her neck, then her throat when her head fell back against the chair cushion. His lips trailed slowly down along the V of silky flesh exposed by the robe's lapels, and his voice grew hoarse. "It's the Talisman emerald I'm after."

Morgan slid her fingers into his thick silvery hair and tugged gently, frowning at him a bit dazedly when he looked at her. "You're after?"

"I mean—it's the Talisman emerald that Nightshade *thinks* I'm after. Can we talk about this later?" He caught her lower lip delicately between his teeth, nibbling, then he was kissing her with unhidden hunger.

She felt his strong hands on her bottom, kneading as he pulled her body against his, and she moaned into his mouth when her naked loins came into contact with the rough denim of his jeans. Without thought, she wrapped her legs around him and her fingers stroked his shoulders and upper back frantically.

He got one hand between them long enough to tug at the belt of her robe, and she felt the garment open up as if it had been designed to slip over heated flesh. Her breasts were crushed against his chest, and the feeling of his clothing against her naked skin maddened her.

She wanted him now, right now, that primitive need overwhelming everything else with a suddenness that was dimly terrifying. She didn't realize her hands were tugging at his shirt until she had to lean back a bit to cope with his buttons, and then the tautness of his face and the blazing need in his eyes told her that he was as impatient for her as she was for him.

Quinn helped her get his shirt off and tossed it aside. He unfastened his jeans and pushed them and his shorts down only as far as necessary, then guided her hips toward him until his hard flesh sank deeply into her body. Her thighs tightened strongly around his waist and her body arched in an instant response, and Morgan heard herself cry out an incoherent sound of pleasure when she felt him throbbing inside her.

His hands covered her breasts, kneading and stroking, and he bent his head to glide his tongue down the valley between them. She clung to his shoulders, feeling the muscles beneath her fingers tighten and relax as he moved, feeling the wild tension inside her body building with a swiftness that stole what was left of her breath and held her in a state of blissful suspension.

When the peak came, it was as swift and sharp as the ascent had been. Quinn wrapped his arms around her and held her tight against him, both of them shuddering under the force of the waves of ecstasy that tore through them . . . and left them drained.

Morgan kept her face buried in the curve of his neck, breathing in the heady male scent of him while her pounding heart slowly returned to its normal steady beat. She didn't want to move or open her eyes. All she wanted to do was hold him like this while he held her, and luxuriate in the sensations.

It gradually occurred to her, however, that their positions, while amazingly erotic, were hardly comfortable now that passion was temporarily spent. In fact, being Morgan, she was suddenly tempted to giggle. A chair in her living room, for heaven's sake, and in the middle of the day. Even with the carpet, his knees were probably giving him hell, and she'd never felt so astonished at herself in her entire life.

He lifted his head suddenly and looked at her, smiling but with fierce eyes. "If you laugh, I swear I'll strangle you," he told her in a voice that was still husky.

He must have felt her repressed humor, she thought. Surely he couldn't have sensed it. . . .

She cleared her throat and tried to stop smiling. "I'm sorry, but I can't help it. I'm not amused because this is funny, I'm just sort of . . . startled. What happened? I mean, one minute we were having a perfectly rational conversation, and the next minute we were . . ."

"Yes, we were. We certainly were." He kissed her, then eased away and pulled his jeans up, zipping them but not bothering to fasten the snap. "Let's do it again."

Morgan found herself pulled up as he got to his feet, and caught her breath when her sensitized nipples rubbed his hard, hairy chest. She wasn't at all sure her weak legs would support her, and when his hands cupped her bottom and held her loins tightly to his, she was sure they wouldn't.

"Wait a minute." Trying to think clearly because something was bothering her, she tapped the middle of his chest with her index finger in a useless bid to get his full attention. "What you told me about your—your sting. You're over here just to catch Nightshade? That's the plan?"

"Mmm," he agreed, nuzzling her neck.

"Then—" She gasped when he gently bit her earlobe. "Then why did you take that dagger the night we met?"

"Camouflage," he murmured. "You would have wondered if I hadn't taken anything that night."

"Oh. Umm . . . Alex? I know I asked you before, but . . . did you steal the Carstairs diamonds?"

"No." He stopped exploring her neck long enough to swing her into his arms. He kissed her hungrily and started toward the bedroom, adding cheerfully, "I just borrowed them."

It was some considerable time later before Morgan could summon the energy to speak, and when she did, her voice held wonder. "Borrowed them. You're a lunatic, you know that?"

He chuckled softly.

Persisting, she said, "You took an awful chance to steal that necklace. You could have been caught. Or killed."

"I needed it, Morgana. Nightshade required a . . . good-faith gesture."

"You stole it for him?"

"I *borrowed* it so he'd think I stole it for him. The Carstairs will get it back, don't worry."

"If you say so." Pushing herself up onto her elbow beside him, Morgan gazed at his relaxed face and said in bemusement, "It's nearly four o'clock in the afternoon, and we're in bed."

He opened one bright eye, then closed it, tightened his arm around her, and sighed pleasurably. "My idea of how to spend an ideal afternoon."

She reached out and began toying with the dark gold hair on his chest. "Yes, but I haven't even talked to anybody at the museum. And when I *do* talk to them, what do I say? I've taken a whole day off, very rare for me, and it wasn't because I ran into Nightshade on a fire escape last night."

Quinn opened his eyes. They were still bright, and very steady on her face. He was smiling slightly. "Do you care if they know we're lovers?"

She shook her head impatiently. "No, of course not. But will this—our being lovers—cause any problems for you? With Nightshade, I mean."

After a moment Quinn said, "Not if I can convince him that I seduced you to get information about the exhibit."

Very conscious of the intent, searching look in his eyes, Morgan smiled. "Is that why you haven't asked me any specifics about the exhibit? So I could be sure you *weren't* after information?"

He reached up and brushed a strand of her glossy black hair away from her face, his fingers lingering to stroke her cheek. "Maybe. It isn't something I do, Morgana. I want you to understand that."

Perhaps oddly, she believed him. For all his charm and his undoubted sexual experience, he wasn't the kind of man who would seduce a woman merely for the sake of gaining information from her. Not because it was a dishonorable thing to do, she thought shrewdly, but because it was the most predictable thing—and Quinn would always choose to be contradictory.

"Sweetheart?"

Realizing she'd been silent for too long, she said, "I understand—and I believe you. I just hope Nightshade doesn't realize that trying to get information out of me in any way would have been useless; I don't understand the security system."

"He knows what your area of responsibility is just as anyone familiar with museums would know, but I think I can convince him that you did provide me with a very important bit of information. That is—if you agree."

"I'm listening."

Quinn frowned a little. "Let me think it through first. Why don't we get dressed and check in at the museum? I know you won't be happy until you make sure the roof didn't cave in today because you weren't there."

"Very funny." But she was smiling. "Sounds like a plan."

They walked about a block away from Morgan's apartment to get Quinn's car, which was where he'd parked it the night before, a distance short enough that it didn't strain Morgan's still-sore ankle. He never parked near the museum when he was being Quinn, he explained to her, so as to avoid having his car noticed.

"That was why you had to carry me all the way last night," she observed.

"Well, it was one of the reasons."

Morgan didn't probe, and she tried to keep their conversation casual. Somewhere in the back of her mind, she had been slowly assembling the bits and pieces of information she had gathered over the last weeks. Discarding some things and reexamining others in the light of more recent understanding, she was trying to put together a puzzle when she wasn't entirely certain what the finished picture was supposed to look like.

It was a slow and rather frustrating process, but one she had to endure for two reasons. Because Quinn was unwilling to tell her all of the truth—at least for now—and because she was too curious to wait to be told. She had an excellent mind, and even if she hadn't been worried about the man she loved, she would doubtless still have been pondering the situation.

But most of the puzzle pieces were still floating

about in her mind when they reached the museum, and Morgan put the matter to one side for the moment. With less than an hour before closing, there were far more people coming out of the museum than going in; it looked as if a respectable crowd had visited today.

"I need to check the security and computer rooms," she told Quinn when they were standing in the lobby. "Just in case."

He nodded, then caught her hand and carried it briefly to his lips in a very loverlike caress. "I'll wander around a bit."

Morgan hesitated, but then smiled at him and made her way toward the hallway of offices, wondering what, in particular, he wanted to examine in the museum. She didn't believe for an instant that he'd be as casual as he indicated, of course. It wasn't that she was *suspicious* of him exactly, it was just that she'd developed a healthy respect for his innately devious nature. She had the distinct feeling that he'd never walk a straight line if he could find a curve or an angle.

She checked the security room first, talking briefly with two incurious guards who reported a peaceful day undisturbed by anything except the usual number of children momentarily lost from their parents and a couple of lovers' spats. Morgan had been bemused years ago to discover that a surprising number of lovers chose to work out their differences in museums— possibly believing the huge, echoing rooms and corridors were much more private than they really were.

Given her own knowledge of the security surrounding such valuable things, Morgan was always aware of the watching eyes of video cameras, patrolling guards, and other members of the public, and so museums were not what she considered either romantic or private.

With that thought still in her mind, she went on down the hallway to the computer room, finding Storm frowning at her computer as she typed briskly.

"Hi," Morgan said, deliberately casual as she leaned in the doorway. "What's up?"

The petite blonde finished typing and hit the enter key, then leaned back in her chair and looked at her friend with solemn interest. "Not much. What's up with you?"

Since she wasn't easily embarrassed, Morgan didn't blush under that shrewd scrutiny. "Well," she offered, still casual, "I'm better than I was yesterday."

"Um. Even after being chloroformed?"

"That wasn't the high point of the evening."

"I should hope not. Quinn?"

Morgan felt herself smiling. "Does it show?"

"Only all over you." Storm smiled in return. "Sort of disconcerting, isn't it?"

"I'll say. And with all this other stuff . . . Well, let's just say I'm taking things as they come."

"Probably best." Then Storm looked more serious. "Jared said they thought it was Nightshade who grabbed you."

"Yeah." Morgan wasn't tempted to go into more detail about the attack; the situation was just too complicated. "Just my luck, huh? Listen, has Max checked in today? I feel guilty as hell about missing work."

"As a matter of fact he's here. Out in the museum somewhere, I think. Dinah's here, too; she's in Ken's office."

Originally hired as an assistant curator for the museum, Dinah was no longer an official employee, but she had come in several times during the past several weeks to help out because she enjoyed the work. Ken Dugan had been unusually busy both because of the new exhibit and because he'd lent a helping hand with the problems of other museums, so he hadn't yet been able to find a replacement for Dinah. That being the case, he had been more than grateful for her occasional help.

"I'll go say hi to her," Morgan told Storm, "and then try to find Max. Um . . . where's Bear?" She didn't see the little cat anywhere.

"With Wolfe—who is also somewhere out in the museum." The computer beeped just then, commanding Storm's attention, and she sat up to deal with the electronic summons. "He's getting a bit nervous. Wolfe, I mean."

That surprised Morgan, since she had seldom seen the security expert rattled by anything. "About the trap?" she asked.

Storm keyed in a brief command, then looked back at her friend with a smile. "No. About a church wedding in Louisiana. He was all for us finding a preacher even before Jared and Dani got married, but we can't do that. After six sons, my mama started saving her pennies for my wedding the day I was born, and I just can't spoil that for her. So, even as we speak, plans are being made back home. And Wolfe's feeling a bit daunted about meeting my family and walking down the aisle."

She didn't sound particularly worried, Morgan thought in amusement. But then—there was no reason she should be. However nervous he might be about the ordeal awaiting him in Louisiana, it was abundantly clear that Wolfe was so deeply in love with Storm, it would have taken a great deal more than a gauntlet of relatives to drive him away from her. It would, Morgan thought, take something absolute. Like the end of the world.

"His job and reputation on the line," she said, "and he's worried about a little rice and orange blossom."

"Men are odd, aren't they?"

Chuckling, Morgan lifted a hand in farewell and went on down the hall. She stopped at her office, discovering that her clipboard wasn't on her desk where she'd left it, then continued to the curator's office at the end of the hall. She found Dinah Bannister there at Ken's desk; the lovely, delicate redhead was just hanging up the phone, and her mildly puzzled expression changed to concern when she looked up to see Morgan in the doorway.

"Hey, are you all right?"

"Fine," Morgan assured her, knowing that Max's wife would be aware of what had happened last night. "Actually, it all seems like something out of a nightmare now, as if it never happened."

"Max said you could have been killed."

Quinn had said the same thing, Morgan remembered. "I don't know—it happened so fast I didn't have time to be scared. Anyway, it's over now." She glanced around at Ken's cluttered office. "Have you seen my clipboard? It wasn't on my desk, so I figured—"

"Is this it?"

"Yeah, thanks. Ken must have needed it. I really should have come in today."

Amused, Dinah said, "Stop feeling so guilty, for heaven's sake. You've been working long hours for months, and an unscheduled day off never hurt anybody. Besides, as far as I can tell, there haven't been any problems."

"You were frowning when I came in," Morgan observed.

Dinah shook her head dismissively. "Oh, I was just talking to Stuart Atkins—at the Collier Museum?— and he told me that several of the museums in the area have been having problems with their security systems. Alarms going off for no reason, things like that. But everything here seems fine."

"Famous last words," Morgan said.

"I know, that's why I'll tell Max about the call. Just in case."

Morgan nodded, agreeing that would be best. She remained in the curator's office only a little while longer talking to Dinah, then went back to her own office to return the clipboard to her desk. Then she went in search of Quinn.

EIGHT

The lobby was nearly deserted when Morgan crossed it to get to the stairs, but she met Leo Cassady about halfway up. The lean and handsome collector smiled as soon as he saw her, and stopped when they reached the same tread.

"Hello, Morgan. I see Alex didn't murder you when he took you home the other night."

She felt a little jolt at the reminder that it had been less than a week since she had officially met Alex Brandon, but was able to smile at Leo. "No, he didn't murder me—but I have a feeling life will never be the same again."

"And it's all my fault?"

"Well, it was your party, Leo. But . . . we would have met anyway, I imagine. Collectors have been drawn to the exhibit in droves."

Somewhat wryly, he said, "Yes, I can't seem to stay away from it myself. Is Alex here now?"

"He's around somewhere," Morgan replied casually. "Max too."

"I talked to Max upstairs, but I didn't see Alex. Tell him I said hello, will you?"

"Sure. See you later."

Morgan continued up the stairs as he continued down, and when she was at the top, she paused to look back and watch Leo strolling through the lobby to the front doors. Even his lazy saunter couldn't quite hide the kind of ease and grace that came from muscles under perfect control, like those of a dancer or an athlete.

What had Quinn said? *If you came face to face with a man you knew was Nightshade* . . .

Nightshade *was* someone she knew. Probably someone she knew well, or at least saw on a regular basis, or else Quinn might have told her who he was. Could it be Leo?

She gripped the massive bannister and looked rather blindly down into the lobby, her thoughts whirling, feeling suddenly very cold. Leo? He was certainly a collector, and though he often made light of it, he had himself termed his hunger for rare and beautiful things an obsession. He had traveled all over the world gathering them, paying incredible amounts to own what no other man could. . . .

Leo . . . Nightshade?

Morgan didn't want to believe it. She didn't even want to consider it possible. Nightshade had killed people—including a young woman of twenty-two whom

Alex Brandon had loved like a sister. Nightshade had shot Alex—Quinn.

Nightshade had used chloroform on her.

As hard as she tried to remember, Morgan couldn't recall any identifying characteristic of the man who had held her in an iron grasp and rendered her unconscious. He'd been taller than she was, but she wasn't sure how much taller. Strong. Quick. She could remember no scent except the chloroform, and no sound except those made in her own struggles.

Could Leo chloroform a young woman he knew well and the next day meet her with a pleasant smile?

Quinn had said something once about having the ability to lie convincingly under stress. He'd said it took a certain kind of nerve—or a devious nature. Did Leo also possess that brand of cunning?

She couldn't know, not for sure. With a faint shiver, Morgan turned and slowly made her way toward the Mysteries Past exhibit, where she expected to find Quinn. She wondered if he would answer with the truth if she asked him whether Leo was Nightshade. She wondered if she could even ask.

"I don't like it," Max said.

"I didn't expect you would." Quinn sighed and eyed the other man rather cautiously. "Look, we both know Morgan's impulsive; I'd made her mad and she came to pour wrath all over me. She was smart enough to figure out where I was watching, and furious enough to come storming up the fire escape."

"I know that, Alex." Max shifted his broad shoulders just a bit in a rare movement that gave away his tension. "What I don't know—and what you've been evasive about—is what Nightshade was doing on that fire escape. If it *was* him, of course."

The two men were standing in a gallery near the Mysteries Past exhibit, out in the open so that no one could approach unseen, and both kept their voices low.

Quinn hadn't exactly looked forward to this interview, but he'd known it would take place sooner rather than later; Max was far too intelligent to have missed the significance of what had happened last night.

As casually as possible, Quinn said, "Didn't Jared explain?"

"No. He said you were too upset to talk about it last night when he came to relieve you. I got the feeling he had a few questions of his own."

Quinn only just stopped himself from wincing. He thought Jared had more than a few questions by now, having had time to consider what Quinn remembered himself saying. *Maybe he got suspicious of me and showed up tonight looking for me. . . .*

It was the only time in his entire career that Quinn could recall having been so disturbed—by Morgan's close call—that he had spoken without thinking. And by now Jared had quite probably reached the conclusion that Nightshade's identity was no longer a mystery to Quinn.

Pushing that aside to be dealt with later, Quinn cleared his throat and spoke in a convincingly frank tone. "Well, it isn't so complicated, Max. Nightshade, if it was him, of course, was probably casing the museum—though I don't know how I could have missed it—and he must have seen me on the roof. I can't know what he meant to do, naturally, but it's obvious Morgan got in his way and so he put her to sleep for a little while. I heard something and came down before he could do anything else—and he left. That's all."

Max never took his eyes off the other man's face. "Uh-huh. Tell me, Alex; do *you* carry chloroform around at night?"

"I've been known to," Quinn admitted candidly. "It's an efficient and nonlethal way of dealing with unexpected problems."

"Does Nightshade carry it?"

"He did last night."

After a long moment Max said, "Is Morgan in danger?"

Quinn answered that with genuine sincerity. "I'll do everything in my power to make certain she's not."

Max frowned slightly. "You didn't answer my question."

"I answered it the only way I could. Max, there are a few things I didn't exactly plan on in all this, and Morgan's one of them. It seems to be . . . more than usually difficult to predict what she might do at any given moment, so I can't be sure she won't charge up another damned fire escape. But I won't let anything happen to her."

"Are you so in control of the situation that you can promise that?"

"Max—" Quinn broke off, then sighed. "Look, after tonight, I'll *know* how in control of the situation I am, and until then I can't give you an answer. You'll just have to trust me to know what I'm doing."

"All right," Max responded slowly. "I'll wait— until tomorrow."

"That's all I ask." With any luck, he'd think of something plausible by then. Either that or else figure out a way to avoid Max until this was finished. "Now, if you'll excuse me, I'm going to find Morgan."

"Tell her I said hello." Max waited until the other man turned away, then added, "Alex? Did you steal the Carstairs necklace?"

Quinn wasn't imprudent enough to conjure a hurt expression or even to sound offended, but he did manage an utterly sincere answer. "No, Max, I didn't steal it."

Max didn't say another word; he merely nodded and watched the younger man walk out of the gallery. A moment later he didn't react with surprise when Wolfe entered from the opposite end and joined him. Wearing his black leather jacket and a faint scowl, Wolfe didn't look much like a crack security expert—and even less so with a little blond cat riding on his shoulder.

But Max was familiar with the appearance (even the cat, since Wolfe was often accompanied by Bear these days). Still gazing after Quinn, he said meditatively, "I'm beginning to think Alex is lying to me."

"Now you know how it feels," Wolfe told him, unsurprised and not without a certain amount of satisfaction.

"I never lied to you. I merely withheld portions of the truth."

"Yeah, sure." Somewhat morosely, Wolfe added, "Maybe Alex is doing the same thing. We both know he only lies about something when he's sure he's going to eventually come clean. If he's lying now, I'll bet it's because he's in deeper than he's told us."

"I'd take that bet," Max agreed. Then he sighed. "And we may have another problem. Mother called. She's in Australia—but she's heading this way."

Wolfe's face brightened, but that instant reaction was quickly altered by a scowl. "The timing isn't exactly the best, Max. Couldn't you stop her?"

"Stop Mother?" Max asked in polite disbelief.

"Sorry, I forgot myself." Wolfe shook his head. "Well, maybe it'll be over by the time she gets here."

"Yah," Bear commented in a distinctly sardonic tone.

Max looked at the little cat and sighed. "Bear, I couldn't have said it better myself."

When he saw her standing at one of the display cases in the exhibit, Quinn paused for a moment and just looked at Morgan. He was vaguely aware that closing time had been announced and that it would no doubt be wise for him to get out of the museum with all speed and without encountering Max again, but he couldn't make himself hurry.

What was she thinking? Lovely face solemn, great golden eyes intent, she stood with her hands loosely clasped together before her and gazed at the Bolling diamond. She was dressed casually in jeans and a sweater, her glorious hair spilling down her back like black fire, and just looking at her made his heart beat faster and his breathing quicken, and caused every muscle in his body to tighten.

He wondered if she knew what she did to him. She'd be aware of the physical response, certainly; he could hardly conceal his desire for her, and so he hadn't tried. But did she know the enormity of it? Did she have any idea that he wanted her, needed her, far past the point of reason?

His life, especially in recent years, had made him adept at hiding or disguising his feelings, but he wasn't sure he had been able to hide how he felt about her. Jared certainly knew, after last night. Max knew, although he hadn't said anything about it since they had talked the night Quinn was shot.

But did Morgan know?

He moved up behind her, instinctively cat-footed because he so often had to be, but she didn't jump when his arms slipped around her. She had known it was he.

"There's a plaque," she said almost idly. "It tells

the story of the Bolling—though not as interestingly as you did."

"Thank you, sweet." He nuzzled her hair aside and kissed the side of her neck. Her skin was particularly soft there, and he loved the way it felt under his lips.

"Mmm. The point is, I didn't even read it. I mean, I helped put the plaques in place for all the pieces, and I didn't even bother to read them."

"You were busy with other aspects of the exhibit," he reminded her, placing another kiss just beneath her ear. Soft flesh . . . bruised by a cruel grip. That bruise still filled him with a hot, almost murderous fury—he had added it to the tally of Nightshade's many crimes—and he brushed his lips very gently over the small area of discolored flesh.

Morgan made another faint sound, then turned in his arms to gaze up at him, her hands lifting to rest on his chest. She was smiling, but her golden eyes were heavy-lidded in the look of sensual awareness he loved. And her voice was a little husky when she said, "We both know how many video cameras are trained on us right now. I don't know about you, but I'd rather not entertain the guards."

Quinn kissed her very lightly. "No, I suppose not." He stepped back just a little, but caught her hand in his and held it firmly. "You do realize the museum's closing?"

She nodded, but sent the brilliant yellow glow of the Bolling a last glance. As they started strolling toward the doorway she said, "Why would any thief want it? I mean, why would anyone in their right mind want to steal something with the history of the Bolling?"

"Aside from its rather astonishing value, total egotism," Quinn replied succinctly. "Every one of the thieves who tried in the past believed they'd be the one to triumph."

"And now? Does Nightshade believe in curses?"

Quinn answered that more slowly. "Nightshade believes he must own what would destroy other men, and he believes he can. That he's somehow immune to the danger. He believes it's his right, his . . . destiny . . . to possess priceless beauty."

Morgan looked up at him. "What do you believe?"

He shrugged. "I believe he's just trying to fill the emptiness inside him, Morgana. He's a hollow man, emptied out of everything that matters." Aware of her searching gaze, Quinn suddenly felt slightly self-conscious. In a much lighter tone, he added, "Psychology 101."

Morgan didn't respond to that. Instead, amusing him yet again with her singular determination to get all her questions answered (it reared its head at the most unlikely moments, he'd discovered), she said, "I checked the plaque for the Talisman emerald a little while ago. "Do you—I mean, does *Quinn*—want it because it's supposed to have belonged to Merlin?"

"Well, a hundred and fifty carats of emerald are worth quite a lot no matter who they once belonged to."

"You know what I mean."

He knew. "Actually, Quinn *has* earned a bit of a reputation for—um—taking items with odd backgrounds or supernatural associations. Not all the time, mind you, just here and there. But it's something Nightshade was aware of. He found it easy to believe that Quinn would have come all this way to try to get his hands on that little bangle."

"And avoid the Bolling?"

"I told him I was superstitious and extremely wary of curses. He believed me."

Leaving the exhibit behind, they walked in silence to the stairs and began descending. Halfway down, Morgan spoke again in a voice that was just a bit unsteady.

"Alex, if I wanted to guess who Nightshade is—"

"Don't, Morgana." He kept his own voice even. "Your knowing who he is wouldn't help—and could hurt. There's no reason for you to know until you have to. Trust me."

Morgan glanced up at him as they reached the lobby, and a little laugh escaped her. "We've already established that I don't really have a choice about that." Then, before he could respond, she was going on in the same casual tone. "You're free until around midnight, aren't you?"

"More or less," he agreed. "I thought we could get something to eat and then go back to your place."

"Sounds goods to me."

After that their conversation steered clear of the exhibit and Nightshade and other troubling matters, and Quinn was glad. He knew he should have kept his attention focused on those matters, troubling or not, but all his concentration seemed taken up by her. She had fascinated him from the first night they'd met, and their subsequent rather intense encounters had only deepened and increased that fascination.

He thought she was magnificent. Not just in her physical beauty, although that could certainly cause a marble statue with no more than the vague form of a man to leave its base and trail along wistfully behind her. No, what Morgan had was much more than mere beauty. She was unusually vibrant, her inner spirit so bright and strong it shone from her golden eyes and seemed almost to illuminate her flawless skin. Her voice was quick and musical, the tone just throaty enough to make every word a caress. And her mind . . . her mind.

Intelligence was only a part of it, though she certainly had plenty of that. She had a sense of humor that was sometimes offbeat and always sharp. A keen perception. More sensitivity *and* sentimentality than she wanted to reveal. And she possessed a deep reserve despite her talkative disposition and charm.

Quinn thought she had been profoundly hurt in her life—and not only by the fiancé too unspeakably stupid to look past her surface shine to the pure gold underneath. She had been taken at face value too often in her life, he thought, and that had taught her to guard her vulnerable heart.

Which made it all the more remarkable that she

could have fallen in love with him. He still couldn't quite believe it. A part of him even considered that if they spent enough time together, she would eventually decide she'd been mistaken in what she felt, but a deeper part of him saw and recognized a luminous truth in her eyes.

He saw it much later that Tuesday evening when he'd reluctantly left her bed to get dressed. It was nearly eleven, and he had to return to his hotel briefly before he could begin his night as Quinn. They had spent most of the evening in bed, and though he hadn't gotten very much sleep during the past few days, he felt peculiarly energized.

Morgan banked pillows behind her and absently drew the sheet up over her naked breasts as she watched him, and in the lamplight her eyes seemed bottomless. For the first time since they'd left the museum, she brought up the subject of Nightshade, her voice calm but deliberate.

"Have you thought of a reason why I would have expected Alex Brandon to be on a rooftop at midnight?"

"Only one," he confessed, sitting on the side of the bed to pull his boots on. "If Alex had told you that's where he'd be. An odd place for a tryst, but I think it's as least conceivable that Nightshade would believe it. Especially since I plan to go on the defensive immediately."

Morgan considered that for a moment. "Because *he* shouldn't have been on that fire escape?"

"Right. And with chloroform, no less. There I was, perched on that roof and studying the museum while I planned a way in for *him*, and he came cat-footing along either to check up on me or else do something a bit more permanent. I'd say he demonstrated a distressing lack of trust in his partner, to say the very least. I'm going to be quite indignant about that, I think. So indignant, in fact, that I'm not at all sure I want to share with him the rather vital bit of information I got from you, sweet."

"Ah, I wondered if we were going to get back to that." She eyed him thoughtfully. "If you expect to sidetrack him that way, it'd better be good. Since I don't know much about the security setup for the exhibit *or* the museum, what could I possibly have told you?"

He leaned over to kiss her, lingering not because he was avoiding the answer to her question, but simply because kissing her had become as necessary to him as breathing. When he finally, and very reluctantly, ended the kiss, he had to fight an overwhelming urge to yank his clothes off and crawl back under the covers with her—and that sleepy, sensual expression in her eyes didn't do much to shore up his willpower.

Quinn cleared his throat, but his voice emerged hoarsely even then. "Why, you told me something only a handful of people know, sweetheart. You told me that Max is planning to break up his collection and donate it to various museums even before the exhibit is officially ended."

She was startled for a moment, but then nodded

slowly. "I see. Once the collection is scattered all over the country—even the world—he wouldn't have much hope of getting his hands on many of the pieces."

"Exactly. With a little luck, the news will at least give him something to think about. And if I'm reading him right, it might just cause him to move a bit faster than he planned."

Morgan nodded again, but then bit her bottom lip as she gazed at him. "Alex, be careful. Nightshade moving faster sounds like a deadly proposition."

He kissed her again, managing to keep it light this time. "Don't worry, sweetheart, I can take care of myself. Besides that, I told you I always land on my feet."

Quinn didn't want to leave her, but at the same time he was anxious to confront the man known as Nightshade and divert his attention from Morgan; she wouldn't be safe until those greedy eyes were fixed once more on the Bannister collection.

It was this thought that enabled him to get up off the bed and turn away, but he had to pause in the doorway of the bedroom and look back at her. Unable to help himself, he said, "I'll be looking for a place to rest my weary head around dawn. Do you have any suggestions?"

She smiled slowly, and that luminous truth was in her eyes. "I believe the lock on the front door is easy to pick. And then there's the window; you didn't have any trouble with it either. It's your choice. I'll be here."

Given that enticement, Quinn knew he wouldn'

have any trouble getting back here. With Morgan waiting for him, the only question was whether he could endure the long hours until dawn.

"Any problems?" Quinn asked Jared lightly when he joined him just a few minutes after midnight.

"None that I saw."

Since they had to assume that Nightshade had spotted the earlier vantage point, Jared and Quinn had agreed—in a brief phone conversation much earlier in the day—to move to a new position and another building. So they met now in a fourth-floor office overlooking the museum, one of several currently unoccupied spaces they had rented before the exhibit had opened.

Keeping his voice casual in what he knew was a vain attempt to avoid a confrontation with Jared, Quinn said, "Okay, then. Say hello to Dani for me."

"Not so fast." Jared perched on a huge old slate-topped desk that had been left in the office by the previous occupants, the position indicating that he wasn't going anywhere for the moment. The room was very dim, but there was enough light to make his expression obvious. Grim.

Quinn leaned against the window frame and peered through venetian blinds at the museum across the street. Well lighted on all sides, the building appeared utterly peaceful. No help there, he thought ruefully, almost wishing for a few armed thugs to storm the place.

"Alex."

"Yeah?" He looked at his brother, still casual.

"I backed you in this from the beginning." Jared's voice was very deliberate. "I bent some laws, and broke quite a few rules, because I knew what it meant to you to put Nightshade behind bars. So far I don't regret that."

"I'm glad," Quinn murmured.

"Wait. I let you lie to Max; I didn't like it, but your reasons made sense. I let you lie to Wolfe, even though I knew damned well it probably meant he'd take both our heads off when he found out the truth. But I will be *damned*, little brother, if I'll let you lie to me."

Quinn didn't move or speak. Familiar with the sound of danger, he heard it in Jared's voice. And though he was an inch taller than his brother, a fraction wider across the shoulders, and arguably more powerful, there was no one in the world he was less inclined to take on than Jared.

Especially when he knew himself to be in the wrong.

"I want the truth, Alex."

"All right," Quinn said quietly. "I would have told you anyway. Maybe not tonight, but . . . soon."

Jared drew a breath and let it out slowly. "Tell me."

So Quinn told him.

During the next few days, Morgan was uncharacteristically tranquil—particularly since she woke up each morning with a passionate cat burglar in her bed. Not that she was calm *then* because her need for Quinn seemed only to grow stronger with every day that passed, but when she reluctantly left him asleep in her bed and went to the museum later each morning, she wrapped serenity around her like a shell.

If any of the others realized that behind her smile and thoughtful eyes a very sharp and observant mind was working, no one said anything about it. Storm teased her about the effect Quinn had on her (she *still* went weak-kneed and dizzy whenever she thought about his lovemaking, dammit!), and both Max and Wolfe had made rather surprised comments about her newfound composure and the lack of chatter around the museum, but if Quinn thought there was anything different about her, he hadn't mentioned it.

That was fine with Morgan. She didn't try to hide the fact that she was in love with Quinn (not that she could—that billboard hovering above her head made it plain); she merely remained calm about it. Almost fatalistic, in fact. What would be, would be.

It was, of course, a deceptive appearance.

He came to the museum every day to pick her up—sometimes for lunch, but always by closing time— and they'd spend the remainder of the evening together, until he had to leave to become Quinn. He was always there when she woke in the morning, though she didn't know for sure how much time he spent in her apartment; he kept his suite at the Imperial and returned there at least once every day. He didn't suggest moving in with her, and Morgan didn't bring up the subject.

But she spent the time with him wisely. They made love frequently and with no diminishing of the intense desire between them. She teased him until he began teaching her how to pick a lock, though he claimed he was only doing it to impress her with the level of skill required. (She was impressed.) And, as always, they talked. Morgan didn't ask him too many questions, but she chose those she did ask carefully and timed them with even more caution. And it might have been because he was increasingly tense about the trap—or sting—but Quinn didn't seem to notice that she was gathering bits of information in a discreet but methodical way.

By Friday, Morgan thought she had figured out at least part of what was happening—and why. If she was right, she also thought she had at last pinpointed the core motivation of Quinn/Alex Brandon, the inner force that propelled him through life and shaped so many of his choices and decisions.

Once she did that, he stopped being *either* Alex *or* Quinn to her; she no longer referred to him by name in the third person when they talked about either of his personas. She thought she understood the man he was now, and Alex had finally become as real to her as Quinn had always been.

By Saturday, Morgan had also reached the conclusion that her beloved was in hot water up to his neck— and not with Nightshade. He was carefully avoiding being alone with either Max or Wolfe, and when Jared appeared at the museum rather suddenly that afternoon just after Alex arrived, it was painfully obvious that there was a very real tension between the brothers.

Morgan stood in the lobby just outside the hallway of offices and watched thoughtfully as Alex stood talking to Max near the guards' desk while, a few feet from them, Jared and Wolfe talked. All four men looked unusually serious—not to say grim—and Morgan had the oddest feeling. . . . It was as if her mind was yelling at her that there was danger here, right in front of her if she'd only *see.* . . .

Then her gaze tracked past them as a movement caught her eye, and she watched as Leo strolled down the stairs. He'd been up at the exhibit, she knew; he visited about every other day as regular as clockwork. He called out something to Max, casually lifted a hand in farewell, and left the museum without, apparently, noticing her scrutiny.

"Morgan, have you— Sorry. Didn't mean to make you jump."

She turned to find Ken Dugan standing in the hallway, and managed a smile. "It's all right, Ken. I've just got a lot on my mind. What did you want to ask me?"

As usual, the curator was faintly harassed. "Didn't you draw up a list of repair people we could safely call for work while the exhibit's in place? People you've cleared?"

"Yes," she answered slowly. "Why?"

"The air-conditioning system. Morgan, haven't you noticed how damned *hot* it is in here?"

Since she usually felt feverish when Alex was anywhere near her, Morgan honestly hadn't noticed. But now that Ken mentioned it, she thought it was a bit stuffy even in the vast, open lobby. "I guess it is, at that."

"I think the thermostat must be stuck," Ken told her. "And since the system's practically as old as the building, I think we'd better have it checked out pronto."

Morgan glanced at her watch and frowned. "I'll go make some calls—but I doubt we'll be able to get anyone out here until Monday, Ken. We'll probably have to shut the air-conditioning system off until then."

Ken nodded, but didn't look happy. "Yes, I suppose that would be best. The weather outside is mild enough, and all the display cases have their own separate temperature-control systems, so we should be all right. Dammit—every museum in the area seems to be having electronic problems of one kind or another."

"Gremlins," Morgan suggested dryly.

He agreed with a sigh, then said, "I'll tell Max and Wolfe, just to be on the safe side."

Morgan returned to her office and made the necessary calls, both surprised and pleased when the second repairman she called cheerfully agreed to come within the hour. It would be time-and-a-half of course, but if the museum didn't mind that . . .

She ruthlessly committed the museum's resources and told the man to come, and after she'd hung up, she sat there looking down at her clipboard with a frown. The Lucite clipboard with its thick sheaf of papers was more or less Morgan's lifeline, containing virtually every bit of information she needed to oversee the exhibit. There was a floor plan of the exhibit wing; design specifications for the display cases holding the Bannister collection; a copy of the insurance inventory of the collection; a long list of people cleared to perform various repairs in the museum should those be needed—and other things.

She was usually careful to leave the clipboard locked in her desk *and* locked in her office whenever she didn't have it, though she hadn't really thought about what information it could provide to someone else.

As she gazed at it now Morgan's uneasiness began increasing. The clipboard had been in Ken's office on Tuesday, she remembered. Why? She'd forgotten to ask him, but now that she thought about it, she couldn't think of a reason why he would have needed any of this information. And . . . Ken had always been around whenever Alex had been watching someone, she remembered.

It seemed ridiculous to even *consider*—but hadn't Alex said that Nightshade couldn't go after the Bannister collection alone? Why would that be so, when he had gone after every other piece he had wanted without requiring help? Was it because he dared not use his own inside knowledge, his own security key card and alarm codes, to get at the exhibit *in his own museum*?

God, how ironic that would be! To have such a prize underneath his very nose and know that if he touched it he risked the police being suspicious of it being an inside job. In that situation, Morgan could believe that the arrival of Quinn would be a godsend. To use that other skilled thief's knowledge, to let *him* find a way past the security—and take the blame for the resulting robbery.

And what would be the risk for Nightshade? Quinn might know his identity, but Nightshade also knew who Quinn really was—and that mutual knowledge kept them both relatively safe from each other as far as public disclosure was concerned.

It was possible, Morgan thought. It was definitely possible. She couldn't imagine Ken gloating in secret over his cache of priceless objects, or holding a chloroform-soaked cloth over her face, or shooting Quinn as they both crept through the night—but then, she couldn't imagine it of Leo, either. In fact, she couldn't imagine it of anyone she knew.

After a while she locked the clipboard up in her desk and left her office, locking the door behind her. She glanced across the hall into Ken's open office, and for a moment she didn't move a muscle. Then, slowly, she headed toward the lobby, pulling on her mask of tranquillity as she prepared to tell Ken that the repairman was on his way.

She thought she'd be able to keep all her thoughts

and speculations to herself. She hoped. But she couldn't help wondering if anyone else had noticed the drooping rose in a crystal bud vase on Ken's desk.

It was only a little after eleven that night when Alex began dressing to leave her, after explaining that he had to return to his hotel briefly. Morgan lay and watched him dress, admiring and unself-conscious. She thought he was beautiful. She also thought he was wired, and even after he'd expended a considerable amount of energy in their bed.

"Is it tonight?" she asked quietly.

He sat on the side of the bed and looked at her steadily. "I don't know, Morgana. Perhaps."

"If you knew, would you tell me?"

He leaned over to kiss her. "Probably not," he admitted with a slight smile. "There's no reason for you to worry, sweet. No reason at all."

Morgan eyed him. "I guess you heard me tell Ken that a repairman was coming for the air-conditioning system?"

"I heard."

She was getting better at reading him, she decided; there had been a flicker of reaction in his green eyes. She was suddenly positive that *something* was going to happen tonight.

"Alex—"

He kissed her again, then rose quickly to his feet. "I'll be back by morning. Sleep well."

Morgan didn't reach to turn off the lamp on the nightstand even though she was physically weary. Instead, she gazed at the doorway, acutely conscious of his absence, and tried to get her thoughts organized.

Tonight. It was tonight. And, somehow, the air-conditioning system at the museum was important. Because it had malfunctioned? Because it had been repaired? She assumed it had anyway; Ken and Wolfe had decided to remain at the museum until the repair work was finished. But if Ken was Nightshade . . .

Morgan had the awful, clenched-stomach feeling that she was missing something, something vitally important. It had nagged at her since this afternoon, and now it was getting stronger, getting unbearable. What *was* it? It had started, she remembered, when she'd stood at the head of the hallway gazing across the lobby, suddenly and inexplicably conscious of danger, as if her instincts or her subconscious had been trying to warn her.

What was it?

She closed her eyes, concentrating, trying to re-create what she had seen in her mind. The men standing in the lobby. The guards at their desk. Leo coming down the stairs. Ken approaching behind her—had she sensed him nearing?

She'd just been watching everybody, idly, not thinking about anything except how grim they looked. . . .

It was then that the final piece of the puzzle dropped quietly into place, and Morgan sat up with a gasp.

Well, for God's sake. *Now* it made sense, all the vague little things that had bothered her all along. Now she understood.

But even as surprise and relief and annoyance chased one another through her mind, another and far more disquieting realization reared its head.

If *she* had seen the truth, then it was always possible someone else had as well. The wrong someone. Because he had her knowledge, she thought. At least her knowledge and maybe more. All he had to do was put a couple of things together, as she had, and look at the sum.

One wrong trick of the light, and Nightshade would know without doubt that he was being lured into a trap.

Morgan glanced at the clock on her nightstand even as she was bolting out of bed and hurrying to dress. Not yet midnight, and it was unlikely that Alex had already reached and left his hotel. Could she make it?

It didn't occur to her until she was in her car heading north that she could have called Alex's hotel, but by then she was halfway there.

She had to make it. She had to.

NINE

The only reason she took the chance, Morgan explained later, was because she was reasonably familiar with the place. She even knew the security code for the garden gate, because she had fairly recently helped organize an outdoor benefit and he had the best garden in town.

Of course, being Morgan, she didn't stop to think either that he might have changed the code (he hadn't), or that security for the house itself would doubtless be much tougher.

In any case, her newly established lock-picking skills were not put to the test. She had managed to make her way through the fog-enshrouded garden all the way to the terrace, but two steps from the French doors she knew led into the study, a pair of strong arms grabbed her and pulled her somewhat roughly away from the door and up against a very hard body.

This is getting to be a habit, she decided as relief made her legs suddenly weak. She turned in his arms and threw her own up around his neck.

Quinn held her for an instant, then yanked her arms down and hissed, "What the hell are you doing here?"

"That's a fine greeting," she whispered in return.

Unmasked, but wearing the remainder of his cat-burglar costume, he scowled at her. "Morgana, dammit, you're supposed to be safely in bed."

"I had to come," she insisted, still whispering. "Alex, I just figured out—"

"Shhh!"

He was so still and silent that Morgan could hear the dripping of the fog-wet ivy climbing the wall beside them. She couldn't hear anything from the house, but he must have, because the tension she could feel in him increased. Then his gloved hands lifted quickly to frame her face, and he gazed at her with such intensity that his green eyes were like a cat's in the dark, alight and vibrant.

"Sweetheart, listen to me. There's no time—he'll be in the study in just a minute. I want you to stay here, right here, and don't move. Do you understand?"

"But—"

"Morgan, promise me! No matter what you see or hear, no matter what you think is happening in that room, you stay here and don't make a sound until you're absolutely sure he's gone. Promise."

"All right, I promise. But, Alex—"

He kissed her, briefly but with such overwhelming

hunger that she felt her knees buckle. "I love you," he whispered against her lips.

Morgan found herself leaning back among wet ivy, shaken and bemused, wondering if she had really heard him say that. She fought to clear her mind, suddenly more afraid than she'd ever been before, because she had the cold idea that he wouldn't have said it unless he thought he might not get another chance.

Her promise kept her silent, and by the time she could gather her thoughts, he had swiftly and skillfully opened the French doors and had gone into the house. He'd left the door just barely ajar; she'd be able to hear what when on in the study. From her position she could see him as he moved draperies aside to the right of the door and reached up a gloved finger to punch numbers on a keypad.

The security system, she realized vaguely. He knew the codes? Well, of course he did. He was Quinn.

Then he stepped away from the doors, and Morgan moved carefully until she could—just barely—see into the room. With the lamplight in there, and the darkness of the foggy terrace, she knew she was invisible to anyone in the room, but she was wary enough to keep her body back and just peer around the edge.

Quinn, his expression perfectly calm and that inner tension she had felt completely hidden, was standing by a fireplace where a dying fire crackled softly. He was still wearing his gloves, and the black ski mask was tucked into his belt. He looked across the room when the hall door opened and another man walked in, and he said with faint impatience, "You're late. If your man did his job, all the guards in the museum should be passing out in another hour."

Morgan was a bit startled by his voice; it wasn't the one she was accustomed to hearing from him. Quicker, sharper, faintly accented, and subtly vicious, it was the voice of a man who could easily be a world-famous criminal.

Leo Cassady, also dressed all in black, walked to his desk and bent forward to study a set of plans laid out there. He apparently hadn't noticed the French doors ajar, or if he did, he obviously didn't care about it. His handsome face was hard and expressionless. "We have plenty of time," he said flatly. "The gas cartridges are set to fire at one-thirty, and we can be at the museum long before then."

"I don't want to take any chances," Quinn insisted. "We have to cut the power in case one of the guards realizes he's being gassed and gets to the alarm. Even though we've been tripping alarms and shorting out electrical systems all over the city for a week, that's no guarantee Ace will automatically assume there's another glitch in one of their systems."

So that's why so many museums have been having problems, Morgan realized.

"We have plenty of time," Leo repeated. Then, head still bent over the plans, he said, "Tell me something, Alex."

"If I can."

"Why don't you carry a gun?"

Quinn laughed shortly. "For two very good reasons. Because *armed* robbery carries a stiffer penalty—and because I'm a lousy shot. Good enough?"

"It's a dangerous weakness."

"Is it? Why?"

"Because you can't defend yourself. Suppose, for instance, that I decided your usefulness to me had ended. After all, I'd much rather keep the Talisman emerald myself—no need to break up the collection. And I hardly need your help now that I have the proper identity codes to placate Ace for an hour or so."

Rather grimly, Quinn said, "I didn't give you those codes."

"No, you very wisely kept them to yourself." Leo looked at him with a faint, empty smile. "But you forget, my friend—I've been doing this a long time. Longer than you, if the truth be told. I took the precaution of cultivating my own source inside the museum—though I didn't sleep with him."

"Who?"

"Ken Dugan. He's such an ambitious man, you know. So eager to please. I'm sure he never saw the harm in discussing the identity codes in the course of a casual conversation about security hassles."

Quinn took a step toward the desk, but halted abruptly when Leo reached into his open desk drawer and produced a businesslike automatic.

Morgan felt her heart stop. The gun, a shiny black thing with a long snout—a silencer, she realized dimly—seemed enormous. She wanted to cry out, to do something. But the harshly whispered warning echoed in her mind. *No matter what you see or hear, no matter what you think is happening in that room . . .* She had promised him.

"This is not a good idea," Quinn was saying evenly, his face expressionless.

Leo walked around his desk, the gun fixed unwaveringly on the other man. "I beg to differ," he said in a polite tone. "I'm not wildly enthusiastic about killing you in my own house, you understand, but it seems the best way. I don't have the time tonight to take you somewhere else, and I won't make the stupid mistake of trying to keep you alive somewhere until I can make other arrangements."

"I hate to sound trite, but you'll never get away with it."

He knows what he's doing . . . please, God, he knows what he's doing. . . .

"Alex, you disappoint me. Of course I'll get away with it. I have so often before. And this time, since I plan to make certain the authorities believe the mysterious Quinn pulled off the robbery of the century, I'll make very sure your body is never found."

"Oh, I couldn't possibly take the credit for something I didn't do. Leo, we can talk about this."

"That's the mistake the villains always make in movies and on television," Leo mused thoughtfully. "They let their victims talk too much. Good-bye, Alex."

He shot Quinn three times full in the chest.

It wasn't her promise that froze Morgan on the terrace, it was soul-deep shock and a pain so great she was literally paralyzed from it. The three shots, so soft, almost apologetic as they issued in whistling pops from the silenced gun, slammed Quinn's powerful body backward with stunning force, out of her sight when he crashed heavily to the floor, and she could only stare numbly at the place where he'd stood.

Leo, sure of his marksmanship, didn't bother to check the fallen Quinn. Instead, he glanced at his watch, then got an extra clip for the automatic out of his desk drawer and left the room with a brisk step.

Again, it wasn't her promise that kept Morgan still until she heard the sound of his car leaving the house; it was simply that the sound jarred her loose from the dark and horrible place where she'd been trapped. With a moan like that of an animal in agony, she stumbled forward, wrenched the door open, and rushed into the study.

"Damn, that hurt."

Dropping to her knees beside him, Morgan stared incredulously as he sat up, pulling his gloves off and probing his chest with a tender and cautious touch. He wasn't even pale.

"You're alive," she said.

"Of course I'm alive, Morgana. I never make the same mistake twice." He pulled the neckline of his black sweater down several inches, revealing a bullet-proof vest. "I've been wearing this thing at all our meetings since the bastard shot me the first time."

"You're alive," she said again.

"Like being kicked by a mule," he grumbled, getting somewhat stiffly to his feet. Then he reached down, took her icy hands in his, and pulled her up into his arms.

She was crying, Morgan realized, clinging to him.

"I'm sorry, sweetheart," he said huskily, holding her very tightly. "I thought he'd probably do that, but there wasn't time to warn you. I'm sorry. . . ."

She could feel where the bullets had struck him, the brutal indentations of the armor plating in the vest, and it was several minutes before she could even begin to stop shaking. He stroked her back gently, murmuring to her, and when she finally lifted a tearstained face from his chest, he rubbed at the wetness with his fingers and kissed her. As usual, when he did that, all she could feel or think about was how much she loved him and how much she wanted him.

Then, with a sigh, he said, "I hate to repeat myself, but what the *hell* were you doing here tonight?"

Morgan sniffed as she looked up at him. "I thought if I could figure it out, then Leo probably could—and then he'd *know* it was a trap."

"Figure what out?"

"Who you really are."

Quinn looked at her with a smile playing around his mouth, then shook his head a little as if in wonder. "You're a remarkable woman, Morgana."

She sniffed again and rubbed her nose with the back of one hand. "Yeah, right."

He gave her his handkerchief. "Use this."

"Thank you."

While she blew her nose and wiped away the last traces of tears, Quinn stepped to the desk and used Leo's phone to place a call. "He's on his way, Jared," he reported. "No, he thinks he killed me. I'll be black and blue tomorrow, but that's all. Yeah. Okay, we'll be there shortly."

Jared must have asked who "we" was, Morgan decided, because Quinn winced and murmured, "Well, Morgan's here." Then he jerked the receiver away from his ear—and she could hear unidentifiable sputtering sounds.

Without putting the phone back to his ear, Quinn merely dropped it onto its cradle with a sigh. "He's going to kill me," he remarked dryly.

"If he hasn't by now," Morgan told her beloved, "then he never will. But you'd try the patience of a saint, Alex."

"I would? Shall we count up how many times *you've* gone charging into danger, sweetheart?"

Morgan dismissed that with a wave of his handkerchief. "What I want to know is—what happens next? Leo's on his way to the museum and . . . ?"

Quinn rested a hip on the corner of Leo's desk and answered obediently. "And—he'll find what he expects to find. That the gas canisters his so-called repairman slipped into the air-conditioning system have laid out all the guards."

"Not really?"

"No, Wolfe got the canisters out after the guy had left earlier tonight."

"So the guards are just playing unconscious?"

"The regular guards are. The extra ones and all the cops are placed at strategic points throughout the museum. Seems they got a tip that someone was going to try to break in, and after finding gas canisters in the air system, they decided not to take any foolish chances."

Morgan eyed him. "I see."

"Yes. So Leo—Nightshade—will cut the museum's electricity, which seems easy enough. He will then call Ace Security and, using all the proper codes and identity numbers, tell them that the system's going to be off-line for about an hour. Which will give him plenty of time to steal everything except the fillings in the guards' teeth."

"He thinks."

"Right. In reality, he'll never get near anything of value, because of a number of very conscious guards and a rather clever little welcome mat Storm designed into an internal security system that Leo knows nothing about."

"But if he cuts the power—"

"The secondary system has its own power supply; it's ingeniously hidden in the basement, and he couldn't find it even with a map."

Morgan drew a breath. "Then you've got him. But . . ."

"But?"

Remembering how they had dealt with another

thief weeks before, she said, "If he never gets near anything of value, then you won't be able to get him for anything except breaking and entering, will you?"

Quinn smiled. "Morgana, all we want is enough probable cause to search this place—something we couldn't get before, because he hadn't put a foot wrong. Breaking into the museum tonight will make the police rather anxious to find out if he might have a few secrets hidden here—which he certainly has. He's got a concealed vault somewhere below, and it's stuffed with priceless things. He's also still using the same gun that killed at least two of his previous victims, something a ballistics test should be able to prove. And if that isn't enough, the police will also find the Carstairs diamonds here."

Morgan found herself smiling back at him. "You were going to get him one way or another, weren't you?"

"One way or another," he agreed. Then his smile faded. "He killed a lot of people, Morgana. And what he meant to do tonight is going to deeply hurt someone who called him friend."

"Max."

Quinn nodded and got off the desk. "Max. Now—why don't we get going? We don't want to miss the final curtain."

They didn't, but as the virtual end of a rather famous career, Nightshade's final curtain was rather tame—and peculiarly apt. The "welcome mat" Storm had cleverly designed had turned a short and unassuming corridor on the first floor of the museum into a literal cage. The secondary security system was perfectly ordinary and innocent whenever the primary security system was in operation, but its activation meant that the slightest weight on pressure plates triggered steel grates to drop from the ceiling at either end of the corridor.

Morgan was astonished; she had no idea that Storm had taken old equipment meant to close off various corridors and had wired in sophisticated electronics to create a cage.

And in that cage, Leo Cassady had no choice but to drop his gun and surrender to the police and guards waiting for him. He was very calm about it, obviously thinking they couldn't hang much of a charge on him. Until he caught a glimpse of Quinn when he was being led through the lobby. Then it must have occurred to him that there was much more to this than he had thought, because he went white.

Quinn, the black costume and bullet-proof vest having been swiftly exchanged for dark slacks and a casual denim shirt he'd had in his car, gazed at Leo with the cool satisfaction of a man who has seen a difficult job completed smoothly.

Leo didn't comment to or about Quinn, perhaps already considering how best to structure his defense in the coming courtroom battle and saving his knowledge of the other man's activities for that. But when the police led him past Max, he paused to look up at the other man.

Leo's hard mouth twisted just a bit, but his voice was steady and without much expression when he said, "If you'd only left the collection in the vaults, everything would have been fine. But you had to display it." Then, calmly, he added, "It wasn't personal, Max."

"You're wrong, Leo." Max's deep, soft voice held both pain and loathing. "It was—and is—very personal."

Leo glanced at the other faces around Max. Quinn was calm; Wolfe grimly pleased; Jared expressionless. And the women, all of whom had been involved with the Mysteries Past exhibit in some way. Dinah stood beside Max, clearly wishing she could ease her husband's pain; the tall and fragile Dani stood in the circle of Jared's arm, dark eyes quiet; Storm was beside Wolfe, her small hand lost in his and her vivid face alive with interest.

And Morgan, who had known Leo best, stood in front of Quinn. Both his arms were around her, and she leaned back against him as she met Leo's gaze with all the steadiness she could muster. She thought she probably looked as unhappy as Max obviously was; her intellect told her this man was evil, but she couldn't help remembering all the times he had made her laugh. She didn't understand how it was possible for him to be the man she had known—and a ruthless thief and murderer.

Then, in a moment that clearly revealed the streak

of cruelty in his nature, Leo said softly to Morgan, "You don't know what he is."

She felt Quinn stiffen behind her, but Morgan never took her eyes off the handcuffed man. Just as softly, she said, "No, Leo. *You* don't know what he is."

Max gestured slightly to the police officers and said, "Get him out of here."

Since Max had managed to get a reliable electrician to come to the museum in the middle of the night and reestablish power to the security system, they didn't have to remain there for long, but it was still after three A.M. when the museum finally locked up again. None of them was particularly sleepy, and most had questions, so Max suggested they return to his and Dinah's apartment for coffee and explanations.

However, the first explanation, the one Morgan had figured out on her own, was waiting for them at the apartment, clearly and justly incensed at having been persuaded by her eldest son to wait tamely for their return.

"As if I couldn't be trusted," she said in annoyance.

"Mother, we've been over this," Max said patiently. "And I explained all the reasons."

"The principal reason being that you didn't want me seen," Elizabeth Sabin sniffed, unconvinced. She was a delicate woman, still incredibly beautiful in her sixties, with a figure a much younger woman would have envied and gleaming fair hair a lovely shade between gold and silver. She also bore a striking resemblance to Quinn—which was explained when he caught her up in an enthusiastic bear hug.

"Mother, how long have you been here?"

"Since yesterday," she replied, returning the hug and kissing him. "I saw Max, of course, and Wolfe last night, but they thought I shouldn't call you or Jared until this thing you're all involved in was over. I gather it is? Alex, have you lost weight?"

"Pounds," he confirmed cheerfully, and caught Morgan's hand to draw her forward. "Meet the reason."

He followed that blithe comment with a more reasonable introduction, and Morgan found herself gazing into the warmly sparkling green eyes of the mother of four of the most remarkable men she'd ever known. Since that was what Morgan had finally realized earlier in the night, she wasn't surprised—but she was still a bit dazed.

"Half brothers, all of you," she murmured to Quinn a couple of minutes later when they gave way for Jared to greet his mother and introduce Dani. "Different fathers, different last names, different lives. But the same mother."

Leading her to a comfortable chair in the huge sunken living room, Quinn said, "How did you figure that out, by the way? You hadn't met Mother, according to Max."

"No, but I'd seen her picture; he has it here in his study." She shook her head and settled onto the arm of the chair when he would have put her somewhere else, adding in a murmur, "I won't be able to think if I sit on your lap."

His eyes gleamed at her. "That's one of the nicest things you've ever said to me, sweet."

"Umm. Anyway, in the museum today—I mean yesterday—I was looking at the four of you, and I realized it was the first time I'd seen you all together. I think I knew then, subconsciously, but it didn't really hit me until later."

"That I looked more like Max's mother than he did?"

"Something like that. You were talking to Max, and Jared was talking to Wolfe . . . and there was something about the way you all stood, or the way the light was hitting you. . . . A bell went off in my mind. Later, when I realized, I remembered seeing Elizabeth's picture here and I thought Leo might have too. I knew Max and Wolfe were half brothers, and I knew their mother had been married several times, so it was at least possible. Leo was smart, he might think of it. If he did, he'd have good reason to doubt that any brother of Max's could possibly rip him off. With that in mind, he'd naturally suspect a trap. It scared the hell out of me."

"Which is why you came creeping through Leo's garden?"

Sighing, she said, "Well, it occurred to me that if Max didn't know it was *Leo* you were after, and he didn't know that Quinn and Nightshade were supposedly in cahoots, then he probably also didn't know that it would be important to make sure Leo didn't find out you guys were brothers."

Before Quinn could respond to that tangled explanation, Max said rather bitterly, "Obviously, there was too damned much that Max didn't know."

Morgan glanced around the room, finding the other beginning to settle into chairs and couches. Dinah and Storm, both having spent the previous evening here getting to know Elizabeth, were handing out coffee to the others. There were a number of expectant faces in the room, and more than one frown directed at Quinn.

Somewhat hastily, Quinn said, "Jared, why don't you start the ball rolling?"

With a faint shrug, Jared did, setting up the situation very briefly by explaining how he and Alex had believed they could construct a trap to catch Nightshade.

"We know that," Max told him, very patiently. "What we don't know is at what point Alex identified Leo as Nightshade."

"Ask him," Jared advised dryly.

Quinn sent him a glance and murmured, "Traitor."

Max, unamused by the byplay, said, "Alex?"

"It was . . . fairly recently." Quinn glanced at his mother, reluctant to mention the night he'd been shot, then hurried on, hoping Max wouldn't demand too many specifics. "I thought I might have some luck if I approached him directly and proposed a partnership. After all, I was a virtual stranger here with no professional contacts, and he had no experience burgling museums because he's always favored private homes— so it seemed obvious a partnership would be mutually beneficial."

"That's not what you told us," Wolfe observed in a tone of dangerous quiet.

Quinn cleared his throat. "I know . . . but just setting a trap in the museum and waiting to see if he decided to rob the place seemed to me awfully chancy. Besides which, he could have waited weeks to make his move, and I didn't think any of us wanted to wait and pace the floor that long."

"So you decided to push him," Max said.

"Well, more or less. After I made contact with him, I assured him I could find a way into the museum, and he wanted the collection badly enough to let me try. And it worked," he added lightly. "He was caught breaking into the museum, and the police will certainly find plenty of evidence they can use against him when they search his house."

Morgan frowned. "But Leo also knows a few things that could hurt you. He knows that Alex Brandon is Quinn." She sent a hasty glance toward Elizabeth, worried that she'd said too much, but the older woman smiled at her with utter calm and Morgan returned her gaze to her beloved.

"Does he?" Quinn smiled up at her. "He *says* Alex Brandon is Quinn. But all he really knows is that I told him I was Quinn, and he can't prove that; there hasn't been a single robbery attributed to Quinn here in San Francisco. If he tries to implicate me in any way, my sterling reputation should protect me. Besides, Interpol will report that the man they strongly suspect of being Quinn never left Europe. And since there have been a couple of robberies on that side of the Atlantic attributed to Quinn during the past week or so—while Alex Brandon was blamelessly over here—well, who would you believe?"

Mildly, Max said, "Lucky for you the Carstairs family decided not to go public about losing their necklace."

In a tone of great innocence, Quinn said, "No, it's just lucky that the police will find that necklace in Leo's safe. Obviously, Nightshade stole the thing."

"Obviously," Wolfe grunted.

Storm giggled suddenly and, to Quinn, said, "I'll say this for you, Alex—you keep your balance on a high wire."

"Practice," he told her.

Somewhat dryly, his mother said, "Alex, don't you think it's time you told your brothers the truth?"

TEN

Quinn half closed his eyes and shook his head.

"Which truth?" Max demanded. "Mother, you knew Alex was a cat burglar?"

"Of course I knew, darling. He told me all about it after he burgled that first place years ago."

Max's hard face rarely showed emotion, but it was clear he was, not to put too fine a point on it, surprised. "You knew he was a thief?"

"Oh, he's never been a thief, Max. You think I don't know my boys? He just created a thief, invented one to blend into all the places where the police aren't supposed to go. Because he knew it would work."

Morgan looked pleased by the information, but not terribly surprised. Quinn had been fairly certain she'd figured out the truth. It was Max and Wolfe he was worried about.

The eldest brother looked at the youngest for a

long, steady moment during which Quinn assumed a ridiculously innocent expression, then turned his gaze to Jared. Whistling softly under his breath, Jared was gazing at the toe of his shoe.

"Jared?"

"Yeah?"

"How long has Alex been with Interpol?"

Jared frowned, deep in thought. "You know, I'm not really sure. Alex, do you happen to remember when you signed on?"

"I've always been lousy with dates," Quinn murmured.

Wolfe spoke up then, his voice sardonic. "I've always been good with my hands. Would either of you clowns like a demonstration?"

Jared glanced at him, winced slightly, and said, "I guess it's been . . . almost ten years now."

Max drew a deep, slow breath, the picture of a man striving not to lose a rare but considerable temper. "Ten years. For ten years Alex has been playing the part of an infamous cat burglar."

"I *am* infamous," Quinn said a bit aggrievedly. "And the whole point of being undercover is that nobody knows, Max."

"Jared knew."

"I had to have a contact. Besides, Jared and I both spent most of our time in Europe, while you two hardly even visited. And when we *did* see each other—well, the subject just never came up. If you'd asked me, I wouldn't have lied about it. But neither of you ever asked me if I was with Interpol."

He looked at his two oldest brothers, encountered dangerous stares from both, and assumed a suitably chastened expression. "It isn't so bad, is it? I mean, nothing terrible happened, so—"

"You robbed people," Wolfe said.

"Well, not exactly." Quinn looked at Jared. "Help me out here, will you?"

Avoiding Max's gaze, Jared said, "The first few 'robberies' were faked with the cooperation of the people involved. After that, it was easy enough to build a mystique around him and let the press run away with it. Every time there was a slick robbery, somebody yelled Quinn. So his reputation grew, and in the meantime he was using his—uh—natural talents to get information and evidence for us."

Max looked at Quinn. "So when you came to me with that lovely story about needing to help Interpol capture Nightshade to keep your own ass out of jail, it was just to *persuade* me to risk the collection?"

Quinn winced, but met that steely gaze steadily. "I'm sorry, Max. I just didn't think you'd do it unless you believed it was to help me."

Jared grunted. "I told him it was a lunatic idea."

"Why didn't you tell me?" Max demanded.

"I *did* tell you. Often."

"You didn't mention my brother was in danger of being locked up." Max glared at him. "Speaking of which, you two must have had a fine time playing the roles of estranged brothers. I felt like a referee half the time."

Jared glared right back. "Hey, we weren't the only ones keeping secrets; you turned out to be a pretty fluent liar yourself."

Wolfe looked at Max. "You did, dammit. Why the hell couldn't you tell me from the beginning that the three of you were setting a trap for Nightshade? You let me believe Quinn was the one Jared was after."

"Just in the beginning—because you didn't tell me you knew Quinn was Alex," Max retorted.

"Until he got shot, I didn't think *you* knew."

"Alex!" Elizabeth scolded, for all the world as if a small son had come home with a black eye.

Her youngest, though far from small, looked a bit sheepish, contritely accepting the blame for having gotten himself shot. "Sorry, Mother," he murmured.

Max stared at him for a moment, then looked at Jared. "All these years you've let him—"

"Hey, wait a minute." Quinn's expression was serious. "My life, Max. And my idea. Jared didn't like it, but he knew I'd go ahead alone if I had to. He made sure I didn't have to."

"Since I couldn't stop him," Jared confirmed wryly, "it seemed best to do what I could to help him stay alive. You wouldn't believe some of the insane chances he's taken—"

"Let's not talk about that," Quinn interrupted hastily.

Wolfe was scowling. "I still want to know why I had

to find out what you were—or were supposed to be—by catching you with your hand in a safe."

"If you'd been in bed where you were supposed to be at that hour," Quinn told him, "it wouldn't have happened. How was I supposed to know that you were Bishop's houseguest?"

Wolfe and Max spoke at the same time, neither being very clear but both obviously still not ready to forgive the beleaguered Quinn. Jared added his piece, defending various decisions made over the years.

Morgan rested her elbow on the back of the chair beside Quinn's fair head and listened in amusement, briefly wondering if there was about to be a glorious free-for-all between the brothers. Or maybe bared bodkins at dawn—if only they could figure out who'd been the most ill-used. Deciding not to await a possible brawl, she laughed suddenly.

"What's so funny?" Quinn asked her.

"Oh, what a tangled web we weave. Looks like all four of you got your fingers caught in this one."

The sun was coming up when Alex and Morgan got back to her apartment, and after the active night and all the coffee, both were still wide-awake. They hadn't said much on the drive back, and it wasn't until they were in the apartment that she was ready to bring up the subject echoing in her mind.

Being Morgan, she made her voice mild and

matter-of-fact even as her entire body tensed in anxiety.

"Will you be going back to Europe soon? I mean, I know Jared said he and Dani wanted a honeymoon before he goes back on duty, but now that your work here is finished—"

He grasped her shoulders and turned her to face him, then tipped her chin up when she would have refused to meet his gaze. His expression was grave. "I have a few more weeks of leave coming to me," he replied. "I thought I might spend the time wisely."

"Oh? Doing what?"

"Trying to make everything up to you."

She managed a smile. "You mean because you lied so much? It's all right, Alex—I know why you did that."

"Do you?" His face remained solemn.

"Sure. In a funny way, you're like Max. Both of you go out of your way to keep the people you care about from being in trouble. In this case, you didn't want your brothers in danger, so you lied about what you were doing. Storm was right, you know. You've got pretty good balance on a high wire."

"I never wanted to lie to you, Morgana."

"I know that. I know it really bothered you, especially once we—we became lovers."

He seemed to hesitate, then spoke slowly, "This may not be the right time, because it's been a long night and we're both tired . . . but there are things we need to talk about."

Morgan braced herself. "Okay."

"First, I think we should discuss this habit you have of rushing into harm's way. Is this something I should be prepared for in the future?"

She blinked at him. "Well . . ."

"I mean, is it because you can't trust me to know what I'm doing, or is it simply your . . . impulsiveness?"

"The latter," she decided, matching his gravity. "Sometimes I just don't stop to think."

"Mmm. An odd trait for a normally rational woman, wouldn't you say?"

"Yes, I suppose—but you're the reckless one, Alex. I have a feeling Jared could tell some hair-raising stories if you'd only let him."

"Don't change the subject," he said severely.

Morgan looked at him for a long moment, then smiled. "Alex, the truth is that I'm *usually* a rational and reasonable woman, and *generally* take care not to do stupid or reckless things."

"But?" he prompted.

"But . . . I've discovered that I sort of like having tense, exciting things going on around me. I'm not saying I enjoyed watching you bleed on my floor, and seeing you get shot last night is probably going to give me at least a few nightmares, but I'm afraid neither would stop me from—um—rushing into harm's way again. I'd still follow a bunch of thugs into an abandoned building, or bolt up a fire escape in the dark, or creep through a foggy garden to get to a house where I know a killer lives—if you're there."

"And if you thought I was in trouble?"

"Afraid so. I can't seem to help myself."

"You realize, of course, that given my job, I will probably be in those kinds of circumstances on a fairly regular basis."

"I imagine so."

"So I'd be foolish to suppose you could ever be a demure and . . . compliant wife?"

"I can be demure if the occasion calls for it," she argued. And then she realized what he'd said, and stared up at him uncertainly.

He framed her face in both hands, smiling just a little. "But never compliant. You're smart, perceptive, stubborn, amusing, and incredibly passionate—and I think I fell in love with you that first night when I caught you in my arms."

Morgan felt herself smiling. "Did you? You were such a scoundrel, Alex, full of charm and danger. I was absolutely appalled at myself when I realized how I felt about you."

"And now?" he murmured.

"And now . . . you're still full of charm and danger. It's the way you're made. I wouldn't change a thing about you, you know. I love you."

He bent his head and kissed her, slowly, hunger unhidden. His eyes were heavy-lidded when he looked at her, and his voice was husky when he said, "Marry me, sweetheart."

As usual when he kissed her, her knees had buckled and she thought her heart had stopped beating, but Morgan managed to say, "I thought you'd never ask."

Alex kissed her again, with delight and passion, and then lifted her easily into his arms and started toward the bedroom. "I want to spend the entire day in bed with you," he told her a bit fiercely.

"Sounds like a plan," Morgan approved, so happy she was dazed with it.

It was much later when Alex stirred and asked curiously, "How did you know it was Leo?"

"I didn't." She cuddled closer and smiled when his arms tightened around her. "I needed to find you . . . and something told me where you'd be. Maybe I have a guardian angel."

"Or maybe I do," Alex murmured.

Morgan thought it was likely.

THE EDITOR'S CORNER

The heroines in September's LOVESWEPT novels have a secret dream of love and passion—and they find the answer to their wishes with FANTASY MEN! Whether he's a dangerous rogue, a dashing prince, or a lord of the jungle, he's a masterful hero who knows just the right moves that dazzle the senses, the teasing words that stoke white-hot desire, and the seductive caresses that promise ecstasy. He's the kind of man who can make a woman do anything, the only man who can fulfill her deepest longing. And the heroines find they'll risk all, even their hearts, to make their dreams come true with FANTASY MEN. . . .

Our first dream lover sizzles off the pages of Sandra Chastain's **THE MORNING AFTER**, LOVESWEPT #636. Razor Cody had come to Savannah seeking revenge on the man who'd destroyed his business, but instead he found a fairy-tale princess whose violet eyes and spun-gold hair made him yearn for what he'd never dared to hope would be his! Rachel Kimble told him she'd known he was coming and hinted of the treasure he'd find if he stayed, but she couldn't conceal her shocking desire for the mysterious stranger! Vowing to keep her safe from shadows that haunted her nights, Razor fought to heal Rachel's pain, as her gentle touch soothed his own. **THE MORNING AFTER** is Sandra Chastain at her finest.

Cindy Gerard invites you to take one last summer swim with her fantasy man in **DREAM TIDE, LOVESWEPT #637.** Patrick Ryan was heart-stoppingly gorgeous—all temptation and trouble in a pair of jeans. And Merry Clare Thomas was stunned to wake up in his arms . . . and in his bed! She'd taken refuge in her rental cottage, never expecting the tenant to return that night—or that he'd look exactly like the handsome wanderer of a hundred years ago who'd been making steamy love to her in her dreams every night for a week. Was it destiny or just coincidence that Pat called her his flame, his firebrand, just as her dream lover had? Overwhelmed by need, dazzled by passion, Merry responded with fierce pleasure to Pat's wildfire caresses, possessed by him in a magical enchantment that just couldn't be real. But Cindy's special touch is all too real in this tale of a fantasy come true.

TROUBLE IN PARADISE, LOVESWEPT #638, is another winner from one of LOVESWEPT's rising stars, Susan Connell. Just lying in a hammock, Reilly Anderson awakened desire potent enough to take her breath away, but Allison Richards fought her attraction to the bare-chested hunk who looked like he'd stepped out of an adventure movie! Gazing at the long-legged vision who insisted that he help her locate her missing brother-in-law, Reilly knew that trouble had arrived . . . the kind of trouble a man just had to taste! Reilly drew her into a paradise of pleasure, freeing her spirit with tender savagery and becoming her very own Tarzan, Lord of the Jungle. He swore he'd make her see she had filled his heart with joy and that he'd never let her go.

Linda Jenkins's fantasy is a **SECRET ADMIRER,** LOVESWEPT #639. An irresistible rascal, Jack was the golden prince of her secret girlhood fantasies, but Kary Lucas knew Jack Rowland could never be hers! Back then he'd always teased her about being the smartest girl in town—how could she believe the charming nomad with the bad-boy grin when he insisted he was home to stay at last? Jack infuriated her and made her ache with sensual longing. But when mysterious gifts began arriving, presents and notes that seemed to know her private passions, Kary was torn: tempted by the romance of her unknown knight, yet thrilled by the explosive heat of Jack's embraces, the insatiable need he aroused. Linda's fantasy man has just the right combination of dreamy mystery and thrilling reality to keep your nights on fire!

Terry Lawrence works her own unique LOVESWEPT magic with **DANCING ON THE EDGE,** LOVE-SWEPT #640. Stunt coordinator Greg Ford needed a woman to stand up to him, to shake him up, and Annie Oakley Cartwright decided she was just the brazen daredevil to do it! Something burned between them from the moment they met, made Annie want to rise to his challenge, to tempt the man who made her lips tingle just by looking. Annie trusted him with her body, ached to ease his sorrow with her rebel's heart. Once she'd reminded him life was a series of gambles, and love the biggest one of all, she could only hope he would dance with his spitfire as long as their music played. Terry's spectacular romance will send you looking for your own stuntman!

Leanne Banks has a regal fantasy man for you in **HIS ROYAL PLEASURE**, LOVESWEPT #641. Prince Alex swept into her peaceful life like a swashbuckling pirate, confidently expecting Katherine Kendall to let him spend a month at her island camp—never confessing the secret of his birth to the sweet and tender lady who made him want to break all the rules! He made her feel beautiful, made her dream of dancing in the dark and succumbing to forbidden kisses under a moonlit sky. Katherine wondered who he was, but Alex was an expert when it came to games lovers play, and he made her moan with ecstasy at his sizzling touch . . . until she learned his shocking secret. Leanne is at her steamy best with this sexy fantasy man.

Happy reading!

With warmest wishes,

Nita Taublib

Nita Taublib

Associate Publisher

P.S. On the next pages is a preview of the Bantam titles on sale *now* at your favorite bookstore.

Don't miss these exciting books by your
favorite Bantam authors

On sale in July:
FANTA C
by Sandra Brown

CRY WOLF
by Tami Hoag

TWICE IN A LIFETIME
by Christy Cohen

THE TESTIMONY
by Sharon and Tom Curtis

And in hardcover from Doubleday
STRANGER IN MY ARMS
by R. J. Kaiser

From *New York Times*
Bestselling Author

Sandra Brown

Fanta C

The bestselling author of Temperatures Rising *and*
French Silk, *Sandra Brown has created a sensation with her*
contemporary novels. Now, in this classic novel she offers a
tender, funny, and deeply sensual story about a woman
caught between the needs of her children, her career, and her
own passionate heart.

Elizabeth Burke's days are filled with the business of
running an elegant boutique and caring for her two
small children. But her nights are long and empty
since the death of her husband two years before,
and she spends them dreaming of the love and romance
that might have been. Then Thad Randolph steps
into her life—a man right out of her most intimate
fantasies.

Elizabeth doesn't believe in fairy tales, and she knows
all too well that happy endings happen only in books.
Now she wishes she could convince herself that friend-

ship is all she wants from Thad. But the day will come when she'll finally have to make a choice—to remain forever true to her memories or to let go of the past and risk loving once more.

Cry Wolf
by
Tami Hoag

author of *Still Waters* and *Lucky's Lady*

Tami Hoag is one of today's premier writers of romantic suspense. Publisher's Weekly calls her "a master of the genre" for her powerful combination of gripping suspense and sizzling passion. Now from the incredibly talented author of Sarah's Sin, Lucky's Lady, *and* Still Waters *comes* Cry Wolf, *her most dangerously thrilling novel yet. . . .*

All attorney Laurel Chandler wanted was a place to hide, to escape the painful memories of a case that had destroyed her career, her marriage, and nearly her life. But coming home to the peaceful, tree-lined streets of her old hometown won't give Laurel the serenity she craves. For in the sultry heat of a Louisiana summer, she'll find herself pursued by Jack Boudreaux, a gorgeous stranger whose carefree smile hides a private torment . . . and by a murderer who enjoys the hunt as much as the kill.

In the following scene, Laurel is outside of Frenchie's, a local hangout, when she realizes she's unable to drive the car she borrowed. When Jack offers to drive her home, she has no alternative but to accept.

"Women shouldn't accept rides from men they barely know," she said, easing herself down in the bucket seat, her gaze fixed on Jack.

"What?" he asked, splaying a hand across his bare chest, the picture of hurt innocence. "You think *I'm* the Bayou Strangler? Oh, man . . ."

"You could be the man."

"What makes you think it's a man? Could be a woman."

"Could be, but not likely. Serial killers tend to be white males in their thirties."

He grinned wickedly, eyes dancing. "Well, I fit that bill, I guess, but I don't have to kill ladies to get what I want, angel."

He leaned into her space, one hand sliding across the back of her seat, the other edging along the dash, corralling her. Laurel's heart kicked into overdrive as he came closer, though fear was not the dominant emotion. It should have been, but it wasn't.

That strange sense of desire and anticipation crept along her nerves. If she leaned forward, he would kiss her. She could see the promise in his eyes and felt something wild and reckless and completely foreign to her rise up in answer, pushing her to close the distance, to take the chance. His eyes dared her, his mouth lured—masculine, sexy, lips slightly parted in invitation. What fear she felt was of herself, of this attraction she didn't want.

"It's power, not passion," she whispered, barely able to find her voice at all.

Jack blinked. The spell was broken. "What?"

"They kill for power. Exerting power over other human beings gives them a sense of omnipotence . . . among other things."

He sat back and fired the 'Vette's engine, his brows drawn as he contemplated what she'd said. "So, why are you going with me?"

"Because there are a dozen witnesses standing on the gallery who saw me get in the car with you. You'd be the last person seen with me alive, which would automatically make you a suspect. Patrons in the bar will testify that I spurned your advances. That's motive. If you were the killer, you'd be pretty stupid to take me away from here and kill me, and if this killer was stupid, someone would have caught him by now."

He scowled as he put the car in gear. "And here I thought you'd say it was my charm and good looks."

"Charming men don't impress me," she said flatly, buckling her seat belt.

Then what does? Jack wondered as he guided the car slowly out of the parking lot. A sharp mind, a man of principles? He had one, but wasn't the other. Not that it mattered. He wasn't interested in Laurel Chandler. She would be too much trouble. And she was too uptight to go for a man who spent most of his waking hours at Frenchie's—unlike her sister, who went for any man who could get it up. Night and day, those two. He couldn't help wondering why.

The Chandler sisters had been raised to be belles. Too good for the likes of him, ol' Blackie would have said. Too good for a no-good coonass piece of trash. He glanced across at Laurel, who sat with her hands folded and her glasses perched on her slim little nose and thought the old man would have been right. She was prim and proper, Miss Law and Order, full of morals and high ideals and upstanding qualities . . . and fire . . . and pain . . . and secrets in her eyes. . . .

"Was I to gather from that conversation with T-Grace that you used to be an attorney?" she asked as they turned onto Dumas and headed back toward downtown.

He smiled, though it held no real amusement, only cynicism. "Sugar, 'attorney' is too polite a word for what I used to be. I was a corporate shark for Tristar Chemical."

Laurel tried to reconcile the traditional three-piece-suit corporate image with the man who sat across from her, a baseball cap jammed down backward on his head, his Hawaiian shirt hanging open to reveal the hard, tanned body of a light heavyweight boxer. "What happened?"

What happened? A simple question as loaded as a shotgun that had been primed and pumped. What happened? He had succeeded. He had set out to prove to his old man that he could do something, be something, make big money. It hadn't mattered that Blackie was long dead and gone to hell.

The old man's ghost had driven him. He had succeeded, and in the end he had lost everything.

"I turned on 'em," he said, skipping the heart of the story. The pain he endured still on Evie's behalf was his own private hell. He didn't share it with anyone. "*Rogue Lawyer*. I think they're gonna make it into a TV movie one of these days."

"What do you mean, you turned on them?"

"I mean, I unraveled the knots I'd tied for them in the paper trail that divorced them from the highly illegal activities of shipping and dumping hazardous waste," he explained, not entirely sure why he was telling her. Most of the time when people asked, he just blew it off, made a joke, and changed the subject. "The Feds took a dim view of the company. The company gave me the ax, and the Bar Association kicked my ass out."

"You were disbarred for revealing illegal, potentially dangerous activities to the federal government?" Laurel said, incredulous. "But that's—"

"The way it is, sweetheart," he growled, slowing the 'Vette as the one and only stop light in Bayou Breaux turned red. He rested his hand on the stick shift and gave Laurel a hard look. "Don' make me out to be a hero, sugar. I'm nobody's saint. I lost it," he said bitterly. "I crashed and burned. I went down in a ball of flame, and I took the company with me. I had my reasons, and none of them had anything to do with such noble causes as the protection of the environment."

"But—"

"'But,' you're thinking now, 'mebbe this Jack, he isn't such a bad guy after all,' yes?" His look turned sly, speculative. He chuckled as she frowned. She didn't want to think he could read her so easily. If they'd been playing poker, he would have cleaned out her pockets.

"Well, you're wrong, angel," he murmured darkly, his mouth twisting with bitter amusement as her blue eyes widened. "I'm as bad as they come." Then he flashed his famous grin, dimples biting into his cheeks. "But I'm a helluva good time."

Twice in a Lifetime
by
Christy Cohen

author of *Private Scandals*

*Fifteen years ago, an act of betrayal tore
four best friends apart . . .*

SARAH. *A lonely newlywed in a new town, she was thrilled
when Annabel came into her life. Suddenly Sarah had
someone to talk to and the best part was that her husband
seemed to like Annabel too.*

JESSE. *With his sexy good looks and dangerous aura, he
could have had any woman. But he'd chosen sweet, innocent
Sarah, who touched not only his body but his soul. So why
couldn't Jesse stop dreaming of his wife's best friend?*

ANNABEL. *Beautiful, desirable, and enigmatic, she
yearned for something more exciting than being a wife and
mother. And nothing was more exciting than making a man
like Jesse want her.*

PATRICK. *Strong and tender, this brilliant scientist
learned that the only way to keep Annabel his wife was to
turn a blind eye—until the day came when he couldn't
pretend anymore.*

In the following scene, Jesse and Annabel feel trapped at a birthday party that Sarah is hosting and they have to escape into the surrounding neighborhood.

As they walked through the neighborhood of newer homes, Jesse's arm was around her. He could feel every curve of her. Her breast was pressed against his chest. Her leg brushed his as she walked.

"Sarah's probably pissed," he said.

Annabel laughed. "She'll get over it. Besides, Patrick the knight will save her."

Jesse looked at her.

"Have you noticed they've been talking to each other a lot?"

"Of course. Patrick calls her from work. And sometimes at night. He's too honest not to tell me."

When Annabel pressed herself closer to Jesse, he lowered his hand a little on her shoulder. An inch or two farther down and he would be able to touch the silky skin of her breast.

"Do you love him?" he asked.

Annabel stopped suddenly and Jesse dropped his hand. She turned to stare at him.

"What do you think?"

With her eyes challenging him, Jesse took a step closer.

"I think you don't give a fuck about him. Maybe you did when you married him, but it didn't last long. Now it's me you're after."

Annabel tossed back her black hair, laughing.

"God, what an ego. You think a little harmless flirting means I'm hot for you. No wonder Sarah needed a change of pace."

Jesse grabbed her face in one hand and squeezed. He watched tears come to her eyes as he increased the pressure on her jaw, but she didn't cry out.

"Sarah did not cheat on me," he said. "You got the story wrong."

He pushed her away and started walking back toward the house. Annabel took a deep breath, then came after him.

"What Sarah did or didn't do isn't the point," she said when she reached him. "She's not the one who's unhappy."

Jesse glanced at her, but kept walking.

"You're saying I am?"

"It's obvious, Jesse. Little Miss Perfect Sarah isn't all that exciting. Especially for a man like you. I'll bet that's why you have to ride your Harley all the time. To replace all the passion you gave up when you married her."

Jesse looked up over the houses, to Mt. Rainier in the distance.

"I sold the bike," he said. "Two weeks ago."

"My God, why?"

Jesse stopped again.

"Because Sarah asked me to. And because, no matter what you think, I love her."

They stared at each other for a long time. The wind was cool and Jesse watched gooseflesh prickle Annabel's skin. He didn't know whom he was trying to convince more, Annabel or himself.

"I think we should go back," Jesse said.

Annabel nodded. "Of course. You certainly don't want to make little Sarah mad. You've got to be the dutiful husband. If Sarah says sell your bike, you sell your bike. If she wants you to entertain twelve kids like a clown, then you do it. If—"

Jesse grabbed her, only intending to shut her up. But when he looked down at her, he knew she had won. She had been whittling away at him from the very beginning. She had made him doubt himself, and Sarah, and everything he thought he should be. He grabbed her hair and tilted her head back. She slid her hands up around his neck. Her fingers were cool and silky.

Later, he would look back and try to convince himself that she was the one who initiated the kiss, that she pulled his head down and pressed her red lips to his. Maybe she initiated it, maybe he did. All he knew was that he was finally touching her, kissing her, his tongue was in her mouth and it felt better than he'd ever imagined.

The Testimony

A classic romance by

Sharon & Tom Curtis

bestselling authors of *The Golden Touch*

It had been so easy falling in love with Jesse Ludan . . . with his ready smile and laughing green eyes, his sensual body and clever journalist's mind. The day Christine became his wife was the happiest day of her life. But for the past six months, Jesse's idealism has kept him in prison. And now he's coming home a hero . . . and a stranger.

In the following scene Jesse and Christine are alone in the toolshed behind her house only hours after Jesse's return . . .

"Jess?" Her blue eyes had grown solemn.

"What, love?"

"I don't know how to ask this . . . Jesse, I don't want to blast things out of you that you're not ready to talk about but I have to know . . ." An uncertain pause. "How much haven't you told me? Was prison . . . was it horrible?"

Was it horrible? she had asked him. There she stood in her silk knit sweater, her Gucci shoes, and one of the expensive skirts she wore that clung, but never too tightly, to her slender thighs, asking him if prison was horrible. Her eyes were serious and bright with the fetching sincerity that seemed like such a poor defense against the darker aspects of life and that, paradoxically, always made him want to bare his soul to that uncallused sanity. The soft taut skin over her nose and cheeks shone slightly in the highly filtered light, paling her freckles, giving a fragility to her face with its combined suggestion of sturdiness and sensitivity. He would have thought four years of marriage might have banished any unease he felt about what a sociologist would label the "class difference" of their backgrounds, yet looking at her now, he had never felt it more strongly.

There was a reel of fishing line in his right hand. Where had it come from? The window shelf. He let her thick curl slide from his fingers and walked slowly to the shelf, reaching up to replace the roll, letting the motion hide his face while he spoke.

"It was a little horrible." He leaned his back against the workbench, gripping the edge. Gently shifting the focus away from himself, he said, "Was it a little horrible here without me?"

"It was a lot horrible here without you." The admission seemed to relieve some of her tension. "Not that I'm proud of being so dependent on a man, mind you."

"Say three Our Fathers, two Hail Marys, and read six months of back issues of *Ms.* magazine. Go in peace, Daughter, and sin no more." He gestured a blessing. Then, putting a palm lightly over his own heart, he added, "I had the same thing. Desolation."

"You missed the daily dose of me?"

"I missed the daily dose of you."

Her toes turned inward, freckled fingers threaded anxiously together. The round chin dropped and she gazed at him from under her lashes, a mime of bashfulness.

"So here we are—alone at last," she breathed.

Sometimes mime was a game for Christine, sometimes a refuge. In college she had joined a small troupe that passed a hat in the city parks. To combat her shyness, she still used it, retreating as though to the anonymity of whiteface and costume.

He could feel the anxiety pent up in her. *Show me you're all right, Jesse.* Something elemental in his life seemed to hinge on his comforting her. He searched desperately for the self he had been before prison, trying to clone the person she would know and recognize and feel safe with.

"Alone, and in such romantic surroundings," he said, taking a step toward her. His heel touched a shovel blade, sending a shiver of reaction through the nervously perched lawn implements that lined the wall. Some interesting quirk of physics kept them upright except for one rake that came whacking to the floor at his feet. "Ah, the hazards of these secret liaisons! We've got to stop meeting like this—the gardener is beginning to suspect."

"The gardener I can handle, but when a man in his prime is nearly cut down by a rake . . ."

"A *dangerous* rake." His voice lowered. "This, my dear, is Milwaukee's most notorious rake. More women have surrendered their virtue to him than to the legions of Caesar." He lifted the rake tines upward and made it walk toward her, giving it a lascivious whisper. "Don't fight it, *cara*. Your body was made for love. With me you can experience the fullness of your womanhood."

She laughed at his notion of the things rakes say, garnered three years ago from a teasing thumb-through of a certain deliciously fat romance novel that she had meant to keep better hidden. Raising one hand dramatically to ward off the rake, she said, "Leaf me alone, lecher!"

The rake took an offended dip and marched back to the wall in a huff. "Reject me if you must," it said in a wounded tone, "but must I endure a bad pun about my honorable profession? I thought women were supposed to love a rake," it added hopefully.

A smile hovered near the edge of her husband's mobile lips. Christine recognized a certain quality in it that made her heart beat harder. As his hands came lightly down on her shoulders, her lips parted without her will and her gaze traveled up to meet the shadow play of desire in his eyes.

"Some women prefer their very own husbands." There was a slight breathless quiver in her voice, and the throb of tightening pressure in her lungs.

"Hot damn. A compliment." Jesse let his thumbs slide down the front of her shoulders, rotating them with gentle sensuality over the soft flesh that lay above the rise of her breasts. She had begun to tremble under the sure movements of his fingers, and her slipping control brought back to him all the warm nights they had shared, the tangled sheets, the pungent musky air. He remembered the rosy flush of her upraised nipples and the way they felt on his lips. . . .

It had been so long, more than six months, since they had been together, six months since he had even seen a woman. He wondered if she realized that, or guessed how her nearness made his senses skyrocket. He wanted her to give up her body to him, to offer herself to him like an expanding breath for him to touch and taste and fill, to watch her bluebell eyes grow smoky with rapture. But though he drew her close so that he could feel the lovely fullness of her small breasts pressing into his ribs, he made no move to lower his hands or to take her lips. She seemed entrancingly clean, like a just-bathed child, and as pure. The damaged part of him came to her almost as a supplicant, unwhole before her wholesomeness. Can I touch you, love? Tell me it's all right . . .

She couldn't have heard his thoughts, or seen them, because he had learned too well to disguise them; yet her hands came to him like an answer, her fingers entwined behind his neck, pulling him toward her warm mouth. He took a breath as her lips skimmed over his and another much harder one as she stood on her toes to heighten the contact. Her tongue probed shyly at his lips and then forced an entrance, her body twisting slowly into his, a sinuous shock against his thighs.

He murmured something, random words of desire he couldn't remember as he said them; the pressure of her lips increased, and he felt thought begin to leave, and a growing pressure behind his eyelids. His hands were drifting over her blindly, as in a vision, until a shuddering fever ran through his veins and he dragged her close, pulling her hard into him, holding her there with one arm while the other slid under her sweater, his fingers spreading over the powdery softness of her skin. A surprised moan swept from her mouth into his lips as his hand lightly covered her breast. His palm absorbed her warmth, her delicate shape, and the thrillingly uneven pattern of her respiration before slipping to the fine heat and velvet distension of her nipple.

This time he heard his own whisper, telling her that he loved her, that she bewitched him, and then repeating her name again and again with the rhythm of his mouth and tongue. He was overcome, lost in her elemental femaleness, his pulse hammering through his body. Leaning her back, bringing his mouth hard against hers, he poured his kiss into her until their rapid breathing came together and he could feel every silken inch of her with the front of his body.

A keen breeze rattled the roof of the shed. It might have been the sound that brought him back, or perhaps some inner thermostat of his own, but he became aware suddenly that he was going to take her here in old man Jaroch's toolshed. And then he thought, Oh, Christ, how hard have I been holding her? His own muscles ached from the force, and he brought his head up to examine her upturned face. Sleepy lashes dusted her cheeks. A contented smile curved over damp and swollen lips. Her skin was lustrous. He pulled her into the curve of his arm with a relieved sigh, cradling her while he tried to contain his overwhelming appetite. Not here, Ludan. Not like this, with half your mind on freeze.

Kissing her once on each eyelid, he steeled his self-restraint and put her very gently from him. Her eyes flew open; her gaze leaped curiously to his.

"Heart of my heart, I'm sorry," he said softly, smiling at her, "but if I don't take my shameless hands off you . . ."

"I might end up experiencing the fullness of my womanhood in a toolshed?" she finished for him. Her returning grin had a sexy sweetness that tested his resolution. "It's not the worst idea I've ever heard."

But it is, Chris, he thought. Because enough of me hasn't walked out of that cell yet to make what would happen between us into an act of love. And the trust I see in your eyes would never allow me to give you less.

OFFICIAL RULES

To enter the sweepstakes below carefully follow all instructions found elsewhere in this offer.

The **Winners Classic** will award prizes with the following approximate maximum values: 1 Grand Prize: $26,500 (or $25,000 cash alternate); 1 First Prize: $3,000; 5 Second Prizes: $400 each; 35 Third Prizes: $100 each; 1,000 Fourth Prizes: $7.50 each. Total maximum retail value of Winners Classic Sweepstakes is $42,500. Some presentations of this sweepstakes may contain individual entry numbers corresponding to one or more of the aforementioned prize levels. To determine the Winners, individual entry numbers will first be compared with the winning numbers preselected by computer. For winning numbers not returned, prizes will be awarded in random drawings from among all eligible entries received. Prize choices may be offered at various levels. If a winner chooses an automobile prize, all license and registration fees, taxes, destination charges and, other expenses not offered herein are the responsibility of the winner. If a winner chooses a trip, travel must be complete within one year from the time the prize is awarded. Minors must be accompanied by an adult. Travel companion(s) must also sign release of liability. Trips are subject to space and departure availability. Certain black-out dates may apply.

The following applies to the sweepstakes named above:

No purchase necessary. You can also enter the sweepstakes by sending your name and address to: P.O. Box 508, Gibbstown, N.J. 08027. Mail each entry separately. Sweepstakes begins 6/1/93. Entries must be received by 12/30/94. Not responsible for lost, late, damaged, misdirected, illegible or postage due mail. Mechanically reproduced entries are not eligible. All entries become property of the sponsor and will not be returned.

Prize Selection/Validations: Selection of winners will be conducted no later than 5:00 PM on January 28, 1995, by an independent judging organization whose decisions are final. Random drawings will be held at 1211 Avenue of the Americas, New York, N.Y. 10036. Entrants need not be present to win. Odds of winning are determined by total number of entries received. Circulation of this sweepstakes is estimated not to exceed 200 million. All prizes are guaranteed to be awarded and delivered to winners. Winners will be notified by mail and may be required to complete an affidavit of eligibility and release of liability which must be returned within 14 days of date on notification or alternate winners will be selected in a random drawing. Any prize notification letter or any prize returned to a participating sponsor, Bantam Doubleday Dell Publishing Group, Inc., its participating divisions or subsidiaries, or the independent judging organization as undeliverable will be awarded to an alternate winner. Prizes are not transferable. No substitution for prizes except as offered or as may be necessary due to unavailability, in which case a prize of equal or greater value will be awarded. Prizes are awarded approximately 90 days after the drawing. All taxes are the sole responsibility of the winners. Entry constitutes permission (except where prohibited by law) to use winners' names, hometowns, and likenesses for publicity purposes without further or other compensation. Prizes won by minors will be awarded in the name of parent or legal guardian.

Participation: Sweepstakes open to residents of the United States and Canada, except for the province of Quebec. Sweepstakes sponsored by Bantam Doubleday Dell Publishing Group, Inc., (BDD), 1540 Broadway, New York, NY 10036. Versions of this sweepstakes with different graphics and prize choices will be offered in conjunction with various solicitations or promotions by different subsidiaries and divisions of BDD. Where applicable, winners will have their choice of any prize offered at level won. Employees of BDD, its divisions, subsidiaries, advertising agencies, independent judging organization, and their immediate family members are not eligible.

Canadian residents, in order to win, must first correctly answer a time limited arithmetical skill testing question. Void in Puerto Rico, Quebec and wherever prohibited or restricted by law. Subject to all federal, state, local and provincial laws and regulations. For a list of major prize winners (available after 1/29/95): send a self-addressed, stamped envelope entirely separate from your entry to: Sweepstakes Winners, P.O. Box 517, Gibbstown, NJ 08027. Requests must be received by 12/30/94. DO NOT SEND ANY OTHER CORRESPONDENCE TO THIS P.O. BOX.

SWP 7/93

Don't miss these fabulous Bantam women's fiction titles on sale in July

CRY WOLF

56160-X $5.50/6.50 in Canada
by **Tami Hoag**
Author of STILL WATERS
A juicy novel of romantic suspense set in the steamy Louisiana Bayou by the author Publishers Weekly *calls "a master of the genre."*

FANTA C

56274-6 $5.99/6.99 in Canada
by **Sandra Brown**
Author of TEMPERATURES RISING
A single mother struggles to balance the needs of work, home, and the passionate desires of her own heart.

TWICE IN A LIFETIME

56298-3 $4.99/5.99 in Canada
by **Christy Cohen**
Author of PRIVATE SCANDALS
A gripping story of two women who find their friendship threatened when they each fall in love with the other's husband.

THE TESTIMONY

29948-4 $4.50/5.50 in Canada
by **Sharon and Tom Curtis**
Authors of SUNSHINE AND SHADOW
"[THE TESTIMONY] is one of the finest books I've ever read." —Romantic Times.

Ask for these books at your local bookstore or use this page to order.

❑ Please send me the books I have checked above. I am enclosing $ _____ (add $2.50 to cover postage and handling). Send check or money order, no cash or C. O. D.'s please.

Name _____

Address _____

City/ State/ Zip _____

Send order to: Bantam Books, Dept. FN109, 2451 S. Wolf Rd., Des Plaines, IL 60018
Allow four to six weeks for delivery.

Prices and availability subject to change without notice.   FN109 8/93